Blauser's Building

by Alan H. Neff

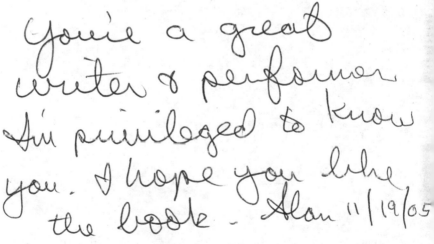

Dear Kent:
You're a great
writer & performer.
I'm privileged to know
you. I hope you like
the book - Alan 11/19/05

Denlinger's Publishers, Ltd.
P.O. Box 1030—Edgewater, Florida 32132
www.TheBookDen.com

Library of Congress Cataloging-in Publication Data
ISBN: 0-87714-349-8

Cover art and photo by
Giau Truong

"The test for abandonment is whether an individual has retained any reasonable expectation of privacy in the object. This determination is to be made by objective standards. An expectation of privacy is a question of intent which "may be inferred from words spoken, acts done, and other objective facts."

U.S. v. Rem
984 F.2d 806, 810 (1993)
Judge Manion, for the 7th Circuit

For my parents Walter and Mary, my wife Meade, my sons Lucas and Liam, and my teachers, who are and were J.H., T. W., D.W., G.M.F., T.P., and F.S.F.

One

Milton leaned his fat little body into the lectern and sweated right through his suit. The high-ceilinged, mahogany-paneled, indirectly-lit federal courtroom reminded him of the cool dark interiors of all the clubs where he no longer could afford to bathe in the music, to scour himself to the bone. Clubs where smooth piano players filled up entirely the long uneasy silences in Milton's conversations with himself.

Next to Milton, leaning as far upwind from him as gravity allowed: Perry Stockbridge, six-foot-five-inches of silver-haired son-of-a-bitch-bastard who was at that moment and in that place beating Milton like a drum.

Stockbridge smiled thinly at U.S. District Judge Sarah J. Forrester. She looked over her half-glasses at the two lawyers and said to Stockbridge, "Defendant's motion to dismiss is granted. There is no conceivable set of facts under which plaintiff might prevail. I won't bore you with my reasoning here. I'll issue a minute order."

"Thank you, your honor," said Stockbridge. He paused, then launched his next salvo. "May I address the issue of sanctions?"

"Briefly," replied Judge Forrester.

Jesus wept, thought Milton Blauser, there is no end to this.

Stockbridge shot his cuffs and glared down, down, *down* at Milton. He glanced at his yellow pad perched on the lectern, at the few words jotted on it, and said, "Sanctions are plainly appropriate here. Throughout this action, plaintiff's counsel failed to advance it, failed to advance his cause toward disposition. He did not cooperate in discovery, notwithstanding your admonitions and great patience. His pleadings were untimely when they appeared at all. This case has wasted the resources of the court and my client. His conduct has been continuously reprehensible, an embarrassment to the court."

Milton stopped listening right then and thought, regretfully, that he should have learned to play the bass.

Minus Blauser's attention, Stockbridge scorched him for a few more sentences. Suggestive throat-clearing and paper-shuffling at the counsels' tables behind Milton induced him to notice that Stockbridge had gone silent.

Milton straightened up as much as he could and said, "Your honor, may I respond?"

"You may, counsel," said Judge Forrester, "but I would have preferred a written response to the motion in the time allowed."

"Judge, I ... " started Milton. And stopped. He passed a hand across the flop sweat on his forehead. "It's ... it's hot in here," he said. A great surge of dizziness, a wrinkling and prickling deformed every nerve end in his inflating body, and his legs buckled beneath him. He sat down on the cool marble of the courtroom floor. He heard but did not feel the side of his head hit the side of the lectern.

Milton closed his eyes, thinking that Stockbridge would look good in Milton's shiny cheap threadbare suits even though they only reached down and out to Stockbridge's elbows and knees. Milton muttered, "Justice served." Let a sigh. Passed *out*.

Two

Todd Brooks's group met on Thursday night th
of Wednesday, which pissed him off. Thursday wa
dammit, not sitting around sucking turbo-coffee wit
lawyers *talking* about the potboilers, page-turners,
fiction, and faction they all were churning out.

Every lawyer in Chicago had a manuscript hidden on
drive at the office. Every last one of them hoped feverishly t.
scribbling, *her* plotting, was a winning lottery ticket; woul
them up forever out of the swamp, the charcoal-gray muck
frequent-flyer-business-class-depositions-in-Dallas-at-daw.
Enshrined in the book-signing circuit, *the* Circuit, the only one that
mattered anymore, they would rise up to join Scott and John, the
Lords of Law, the *Gods*, the first to figure out that the public
loathed lawyers, *detested* them, but loved *reading* about them,
insatiably and indiscriminately.

All the lawyers who made it on The Circuit shoveled it up, their
steaming hot death-slop buckets of blood and barratry — lawyers,
guns and money; lawyers, drugs and sex — for the tabloid-
dependent masses. *And* they got the agents and the publishers and
the six-book contracts and the four-movie deals and the little
rectangular ad signs above the key-scarred windows on the El
shouting the magic incandescent message above their titles: "*The
New York Times Bestseller!*". The New York Times Bestseller
List, the Grail, satori, nirvana, the lock on social status that
surpasseth understanding.

Oh *god*, how Todd craved to see that little ad on the El with *his*
name on it

John and Scott and all the other bile-inducing success stories got
there, had the discipline, the persistence, the whatever the hell it
was, the ... *grit*, that Todd didn't. They had luck, too. All the luck
in the world. Without luck there was nothing, except Branch
Rickey and Todd Brooks knew that luck was the residue of design,
and Todd had none of that, either.

For the 487th time in that month alone, Todd wondered why the
worst was so, why he could fill a regular goddamn *landfill* with
trash-lawyer books that held the public eye like a bloody dancing
cobra swaying in front of some doomed jungle rodent. Trash by

Why was nothing by him in that landfill? He
had skated through high school, college, and law
points, avoiding content because it scared him half
appling with content invited failure, required
and his professors had been entertained enough, just
let him slide.

ily needed a Hook, a good goddamn Hook. Hook the
e the sale. No, he needed a *harpoon*, a mighty mother-
g harpoon that would pierce and hold and *land* the great
whale, no questions asked.

Three

As Milton's eyes flickered open and his vision settled, he reassured President Lincoln that he, Milton, was all right. Almost but not quite soon enough, he realized that Mr. L. was only a Matthew Brady photograph on the wall of Judge Forrester's chambers. The judge herself sat behind her desk watching him, her hands steepled in front of her. At her side stood her chronically belligerent minute clerk, unhappy about ranking as only the second toughest black female in the Kluczynksi Federal Building since Sarah Forrester got up on the bench and deployed the federal sentencing guidelines to terrorize all the white collar criminals who had the appalling luck to draw her on the assignment wheel without an imminently fatal disease or Nobel Peace Prize to shoehorn into their pre-sentencing reports.

Milton sat up. "I'm sorry," he said, adding "your honor," when he remembered where he was.

The judge asked, "Should I call your doctor? Are you all right, really?"

"No," said Milton, "he's, he's, out of the country." Out of Milton's country, anyway. Milton's doctor had stopped taking his calls when Milton stopped paying his bills. Perfect symmetry in the professional class.

Milton said, "I fainted," because it was safe, obvious, non-committal.

Judge Forrester looked at the small clock on her desk, and said "For just a few seconds, actually. There was a doctor in the courtroom, on another matter, fortunately." As she gazed at him — impassively — Milton wondered whether she would end every sentence with an adverb. Predictably.

The judge said, "He had to leave, but he said I should ask you if this has happened before."

Milton waited for another adverb. Briefly. Futilely. When it didn't appear, he said, "No. It was a hard night," sleeping, he added to himself, or more accurately *not* sleeping, on the wreckage of his practice.

"Well," said Judge Forrester, "I called an ambulance."

"No!" He said "no" again, more quietly. Struggled to rise to a sitting position on the overstuffed brown leather couch. "Please, no ambulance. I'm better."

Milton wouldn't get in an ambulance while he was conscious. He couldn't pay for it, and his father had died in an ambulance smashed jelly-flat by an eighteen-wheeler running a red light in Hammond, Indiana, as the ambulance hauled Blauser the Elder from the steel-plant summer picnic where he'd broken his leg sliding into second base in the company's annual 16-inch softball game.

"Would you like a glass of water?" asked the Judge.

"No, no. I'm fine." Milton made a show of looking at his watch but discovered he wasn't wearing one, so he flicked his hand across his wrist, which made him worry the judge would think he was brushing away imaginary flies. "Have to meet a client. Yes. At my office. Right away. Thank you. For your help." He paused, spoke again. "We went to law school together."

"Really?" She smiled. "It is a small town, isn't it?"

"Well, not really together. We didn't know each other." He let his mouth carry him into absolutely forbidden territory. "You've done so well," he said. "It's good. I always thought you were nice."

The judge ceased to smile and looked away from him, out her window and over the Lake. She turned back to him. "Well, that's very kind of you." She stood up.

Milton forced himself to stand, too, and saw his briefcase by his feet. "I have to go," he said. He reached down for it, his cardboard belt biting into his gut, and started to waddle toward the door, hoping he'd get the hell out of that room before he said or did anything else disgraceful. He said again, "I have to go."

The judge nodded and said, "Oh, Mr. Stockbridge asked you to call him to set a new date for his sanctions motion. Let my clerk know then, won't you?"

Bowing slightly, Milton wheezed, "Certainly, your honor." With a weak little wave, he wobbled out of Judge Sarah Forrester's chambers in the United States District Court for the Northern District of Illinois (Eastern Division), the magic land of lifetime tenure, leaving her to remark, sadly and ever so briefly before turning her attention to lighter, merely legal matters, that Milton Blauser had sunk to carrying his papers to court in a canary-yellow, shiny plastic briefcase.

Four

While Milton walked westward the sixteen blocks to his dingy office at 1138 West Madison, above a shuttered breakfast grill where cockroaches outnumbered oxygen molecules, Todd Brooks's support group convened in neutral territory, for dinner and support before returning to their offices for another helping of work.

They met at Mickey's River North, a nouvelle bistro, a culinary oxymoron built to cater to MBAs from Duke University, situated in an entire neighborhood slick with such slime. Mickey's presented French food with a southern accent in microscopic portions, a walk-in humidor, and 75-year-old armagnacs, all presided over by 38-year old Mickey Stein, who'd cooked for 14 different restaurants in nine years after graduating from the Culinary Institute of America, starting, purposefully, if inexplicably, with a Greek sub joint named Hero's Gyros.

Todd's support group consisted of people like him: Louise and Damian and Ed and Mark and JudyJudyJudy, who *adored* Cary Grant, whom he detested even more than he hated hearing them call their little *klatsch* a "support group," which made him feel like a one-day-at-a-timer. They were six-count-'em-six graduates of the nation's most eminent law schools, where they served in a senior editorial capacity on the primary law review and repeatedly engaged with impunity in acts of "legal scholarship" that were neither. Fast-tracking to summer clerkships at giant firms, they were wined, dined, toasted, and encouraged at the partners' picnics to take one or even two federal clerkships. When they landed later on the flight decks of the giant firms as associates, they were treated like pedophiles at a PTA convention, all the while making obscene amounts of money they had not the time, energy, conscience or creativity to spend on anything except 4-star restaurants, natural-fabric wardrobes, and hundred-dollar haircuts.

In all, these were the same caste of clowns who in law school extolled the "intellectual rigor of securities law" with the palpable, painful sincerity of the naive, disinguous, or brain-damaged. And here they hung at Mickey's, intellectually tested, and bested, by spittle-spewing senior partners, mind-numbing document searches, endless editorial meetings at 4 a.m. about discovery pleadings. Veins bulging from the pressure of fear and greed, ululating every day at ultrasonic frequencies behind their closed office doors, they keened: "Get me out! Get me out! Get me *out!*"

So ... Write, write, write. They did that. Network, network, network. They did that, too. And whine, whine, whine. Todd was *right* on it.

Their plan: get the hell *out*. But not without locking up a public sector sinecure that left them time to get a life, if they had the wits still to recognize one and the social graces left to manage it.

Todd was *not* right there. Not yet.

His group had met and bonded at a "writer's workshop" that was 57 parts motivational seminar and one part active-voice exercise. "'He writes books.'" snarled their workshop leader, a copy-editor at Machine Tool, a trade-rag roper suffering delusions of literary lion-hood as intense as the fever afflicting his sniveling student-suckers. "*Not*, 'Books are written by him.' Okay?"

After the workshop ended, Todds and Louise and Damian and Ed and Mark and JudyJudyJudy vowed to meet and did, and egged each other on. They read each other's excerpts, gave aid and comfort and praise to each little reader at each little reading.

But, *but*, before each meeting, they each mailed themselves their pages to be read on that date, registered and return receipt requested and kept unopened, to ensure that no other over-educated, panic-driven parasite feeding in and on the group could ever, *ever*, plagiarize their work and get away with it.

Not suckers. Not anymore.

Five

The two-story red-brick in which Milton officed and subsisted was built shortly after the Chicago Fire, on west Madison Street, an area long since abandoned by business arsonists to hookers, drunks and crackheads. The Health Department shut the breakfast grill on the first floor approximately 15 minutes after Milton closed on the building.

In the 16 succeeding years, Milton tried to entice another business into the storefront, but failed except for three delightful months. His tenant's bookmaking operation closed abruptly and permanently, because the mice ate all its active betting slips, or so the bookie told his silent senior partner. The unsettled matter was whether the mice also ate the bookie, because he was never seen again.

Milton pushed open the street door and slowly climbed the staircase to the second floor, crushed malt-liquor cans and broken wine bottles and used condoms shifting minutely on each rotting step. He left his key in the hallway door to his office, hanging from the rusted padlock that functioned as his entire home/office security system.

He shut the door behind him and put his briefcase up against it. He took off his suit and hung it with all the others on a wheeled rack he found abandoned in a Salvation Army parking lot. From the top of one of the stacks of files rising from the floor to his shoulders, he pulled about forty leaves of paper. Milton carefully spread them on the floor and lay down on them in his tattered boxer shorts and undershirt. He covered himself in his sleeping bag and rested his head on his briefcase.

No heat, light, phone. No prospects or demands. This, thought Milton, is my life, yes. There would be a problem in the winter when it got cold again, but he'd deal with it. He'd deal with it. He'd get through it. Milton curled into a fetal position and rocked himself to sleep.

Six

Clutching their armagnacs or cigars or both (and sometimes both in the same hand), Todd and Louise and Damian and Ed and Mark and JudyJudyJudy lounged at table at Mickey's, dinner over, all of them cranking up slowly to the night's imminent reading.

Louise Melville was the evening's featured artiste, which was *major* ok from Todd's point of view. With legs as long as the Ice Age — and eyes as cold — she could be counted on to dispense fervent sexual favors in a shared cab immediately after their group adjourned, to whichever male praised her work most, and most credibly. Todd and Damian and Ed and Mark reached an unspoken consensus that positive feedback to Louise, however unjustified on a given night, was a small price to pay for access to her lean and hungry body. On her part, Louise had long since made a separate peace with her virtue, sacrificed to these rutting philistines as long as she could stand it, because their comments, however crude and uninformed, kept her writing, and she couldn't call herself "a *writer*" if she wasn't *writing*.

Her five pages for that night, sharply folded longitudinally, lay in front of her as she steeled the nerve she needed and manfully, oops, womanfully, suppressed her disgust at the thought of coupling later with one of these narcissistic pigs who squandered their white-bread high school years pissing-drunk and laid out flat on suburban golf course greens throughout the heartland, groping grunting losers who wouldn't have swum the Hellespont to save their own souls.

Mark said, "Can we get a move on? I have to go back to the office. Numb Nuts wants me to explain, *needs* me to reassure him why I'm right. Why Judge Moron'll agree with me tomorrow." He sighed. "At least three more times tonight."

Todd thought he smiled at Louise as broadly as he could without obviously leering and said, "Hit us with your deathless."

Louise began to read. Like most humans, she normally spoke at the rate of approximately 100 words per minute. She slowed down when she read, trying to tune each word she'd written to bear just the emphasis she intended a reader to take from it, knowing all the while that it was hopelessly beyond her to write it or read it like she felt it and meant it.

The other five listened and looked at her, or away into space. They heard her as they always did, with one ear to her words and the other to the rising and falling conversational buzz around them, hoping to catch from nearby diners just the perfect line they could use.

When she finished, the group reacted, except for Todd. He'd gotten drunk on the excuse of an unsettling success that day and lost his hormonal edge. But he retained enough of a strategic overview of Louise's potential for another night to keep his mouth shut and not burn any critical bridges he might want to cross at a later date, in a cab with her.

Louise listened only to JudyJudyJudy, who was known to be strictly heterosexual and not likely to make a pass at Louise, and, for a change, to Mark, too. His command performance at the office that night put him out of the running for an orgasmectomy. She was pleased and surprised that he was so positive about her work when his mind was plainly unwarped by testosterone overload.

At ten, they all rose to leave. As they walked out of Mickey's, Mark flipped his cell phone open and dialed his voice mail. He announced with relief that Numb Nuts — weakly sensing a looseness in his nerveless nether region — had decided to ask for a continuance. "I don't have to succor the sucker after all."

Louise, in a state of critically acclaimed arousal, immediately linked arms with him and fairly dragged him into the first taxi at the cab stand. As their taxi pulled away and Louise half-gainered out of sight, Mark contrived to wink at Todd, who emerged from his alcoholic haze in that sharp and singular moment to remember that Mark had told him that morning, *that morning*, that Numb Nuts had taken the week off to vacate in Paris.

Todd could only hope, in a furry, fuzzy kind of way, that next morning he'd recall enough of the night to call Mark. To congratulate him on his fucking tactical genius and his tactical fucking genius.

As Todd staggered home, he was sure he'd write this down. This one was a *keeper*. He just had to make all these keepers fit together. Just had to.

Seven

At the north end of LaSalle Street inside the Loop, in the world headquarters of Danville & Williamston, Perry Stockbridge's partners knew that the evil he did would live after him, and the good would be interred with his bones, if he ever accidentally did any. Nurtured in Perry's careful program of breeding, feeding, and culling, his herd of privately-held acronymous transnational clients trampled, gouged, poisoned, mauled, and malled the global countryside, from Pole to Pole, from Kathmandu to Kankakee, merging, acquiring, divesting, downsizing, right-sizing, getting and spending. Old-growth forests were slaughtered daily to manufacture letterhead and bond for the mountains of pleadings fired off, over Stockbridge's signature, in defense of slaughtering old-growth forests.

His partners also agreed that it was, well, ha-ha, kind of, you know, *quirky*, that Perry kept his client list and retainer agreements in a burn-bag. But Perry's prized stable of corporate cash-cows docilely submitted each month to multi-million-dollar milkings, and the pouring of money on second thoughts is the fastest way to extinguish them.

Stockbridge rarely visited The Kennel — his six associates' offices — and less frequently complimented their tenants, so Todd Brooks was badly rattled when the Emperor of Billable Hours filled up his office doorway to say, "Todd," and to praise him: "Excellent job on the Blauser motion." And, so as not to be mistaken for someone other than Perry Stockbridge, to bury him: "You got in a bit later than usual. I hope you didn't celebrate too much last night."

Todd unsteadily maneuvered a weak smile around the sharp corners of his hangover and said, "I'll survive."

"Where are you on the revisions to the requests to admit for AgriNaut?"

"I just finished them. I'll send them to the printer and bring them by." He tapped a few keystrokes.

Stockbridge nodded. "Come to the meeting at ten to take notes. And run up a draft of a complaint letter to the A.R.D.C., please, for my luncheon reading. On Blauser. Just facts for now. Follow the sanctions motion. "By ... " he consulted his watch, " ... 12:30." We'll discuss the editorial content tonight. Seven, say?"

Stockbridge left. Todd collapsed into his chair, nodding and smiling and sweating and seething. You *bastard*, thought Todd. You'll make me wait 'til nine tonight because I was late today, won't you?

Todd's rage instantly dispelled his hangover. He put the sanctions motion on his screen and stared gloomily at it. He sneered at the document on the screen, too, but perfunctorily, without conviction.

A complaint to the Attorney Registration and Disciplinary Commission on that mope Blauser hardly seemed worth the effort. It wasn't billable, either.

To his screen, Todd said, "Counselor Blauser. *Fly*speck Blauser." Hopeless, because he is hapless. Hapless because he is hopeless. But for fear and greed, mused Todd, there go I.

In Perry Stockbridge's corner office, on the screen of the computer on which he never actually deigned to compose anything, Perry watched Todd switching screens, calling up his "Booklines" file, saving his poignant observations about Milton Blauser. The associate seeded his pleading drafts with these mutant epigrams, reshaped most often into calumny hurled at adversaries, but still recognizable.

It might have comforted Todd to know that Perry Stockbridge — his invisible, secret, silent observer — relished the unscheduled resurrections of these heavily edited *bon mots*. Infrequently, Perry concluded that one of them *worked*, and he'd mark a small, neat check in the right-hand margin next to it, causing Todd to wag his behind in gratitude.

Someday soon, Perry knew, he'd miss Todd's bracing brand of battery-acid, but the lad was rapidly exhausting his value to the firm, and there was no question he'd be a dead loss as a partner. Todd could not be trusted to speak in the presence of clients and was incapable of generating business. He did not play squash, and he shot in the high 90's at the firm golf outings. Hysterical on the putting greens and unraveling into paranoia everywhere else, Todd was surely arcing, *accelerating*, into frantic self-pity and inefficient empathy.

Todd's decline reminded Perry it was a waste of time and money recruiting the shoddy spawn of land-grant-universities, ill-considered public monuments thrown up by frightened 19th century legislators to pacify populist agitators and employ their bowling-alley architects. Stockbridge vowed to stand fast at the next hiring committee meeting and put a stop to it.

Eight

Milton shivered and twitched and mumbled in his sleep. His eyes fluttered open at 9:48 a.m, and he calculated that he'd lived and slept in that room for exactly eight years or 2,922 days.

An anniversary. Hurray!

Out of a cardboard box, Milton selected black socks, fresher underwear and a tee shirt. Off a hanger on the rack, he pulled a pair of white pants and a white jacket that buttoned from the neck to the waist. The hanger clattered to the floor, and he squatted to pick it up. He put these clothes in a shopping bag with soap, razor, toothbrush, and toothpaste.

He had to hustle to get to Grant Park before the public showers closed at 11 a.m.. He barely made it, so he wore his clothes into the shower, washed himself and the clothes all at once, and changed into his dry clothes. As always, he stopped at the main post office to check his box before he headed west, back to his office, to hang up his wet garments, pick through the ruins of his law practice, walk two blocks south and four blocks east to Halsted, to Athena's Arms in Greektown, shovel down his daily one free order of potatoes and moussaka, and start his eight-hour shift as a busboy on the front end of the lunch rush.

This was his routine five days a week, and he should have had *some* weight loss to show for all that walking. Pardon the expression, Milton, but fat chance.

In his post-office box, which he acquired because two letter carriers on their appointed rounds had been murdered for welfare checks and their union got his entire block stricken from the delivery route, he found a notice from the A.R.D.C. about the imminent increase in his annual registration fee. There also was a "Final Redemption Notice" from the county treasurer about his property tax bill.

The notice explained the tax sale process — how someone could bid to buy his building for the unpaid property taxes, and had, and that he'd had a certain amount of time to "redeem" it by paying the back taxes, with interest and penalties, but that time was about to run out. The letter also said that if he needed more information or someone to translate the letter or wanted to work out an installment payment plan, he could call the treasurer's office at a certain number between 8 a.m. and 4:30 p.m. five days a week. He turned it over and read the same text in Spanish, which he'd learned from the busboys at Athena's Arms.

"A very clear letter," Milton said to himself. "A model of concision. But where are ... " he ran his finger down to the "Due and Owing" line, "... $9,418.00?" He leaned against the wall of boxes, closed his eyes. Within seconds, he was snoring softly. He started awake and race-walked the two-mile route back to his office, dropped off his stuff and jogged to the restaurant, 12 minutes late for his shift.

After a spirited round of pleading and glowering and frowning and thoughtful jaw-pulling, Spiro Vassilopoulos, the owner, decided that he wouldn't dock Milton's pay, *if* the little man explained how Spiro could make his king-hell bitch of an ex-wife spend his child-support payments on supporting their children and not her fucking little brat by a certain fucking used car salesman in Des Plaines who might have been mistaken once upon a time for Spiro's little brother and former partner Athanasios, except no brother of Spiro, no *hon*orable person, would commit such *"Fucking treachery!"* shouted Spiro, startling a nearby party of three gay cabin attendants who were sharing the "Dinner For ?" Option #1 platter of stuffed grape leaves, broiled white fish, and chicken riganati (all white meat, $1.00 extra per person).

Later, on a sea of ouzo, Milton's after-hours private seminar on family law capsized suddenly and sank. Spiro, slobbering, sobbing, and cursing, unable to *stand* it anymore, slipped Milton twenty bucks out of his own pocket — *"Not the till, my own pocket, because you are a man, Milton Blauser, and not a treacherous fucking bastard!!!* — and told him to *"Get out, Goddammit!!!"*

Milton hurried out of the restaurant before Spiro started breaking things, or him. Feeling flush, he spent five dollars on a cab back to his building, because he was sober and did not want to die, not that night. Milton figured this money from Spiro was a *sign*. He was on his *way!*

He lightly sprung up the steps to his office, unlocked the door, locked it behind him for the first time in months, put the money where it would be safe enough to confound any of his crack-addled neighbors, hung up his clothes, spread out his paper and went to bed.

It felt good to be lying there, safe and warm and dry and fifteen dollars closer to redeeming his building. Milton realized he'd have to put the pedal to the metal, enlarge and accelerate the cash flow, starting the next morning, on day 2,923. He doubted the county treasurer would let him accumulate and pay the other $9,403.00, at 15 dollars a day, in 626.86667 days. That would put him 596.86667 days beyond the expiration date for the redemption period.

Milton rounded down to 596 days, just to be conservative, to kind of spur him on. Stimulated, he began working through his options alphabetically, skipping abduction, arson, assault, bank robbery, bomb threats, bribery, burglary, carjacking, and car theft.

Long-dormant brain cells began flickering and calling out to each other, searching for siblings in the dark abandoned warehouse that once had been Milton's cerebral cortex. Just before he fell asleep, he wondered who was stupid enough to buy the building he'd been too stupid to resist eight years ago.

He sat up, eyes opening, widening. Wait a minute. *He* wasn't stupid. And maybe someone else who wasn't any dumber wanted the building. *His* building.

Nine

It was 10:44 p.-fucking-*m*. when Perry granted Todd his audience, even later than Todd had predicted. Stockbridge sat at the end of his conference table, and he motioned to Todd to stand beside him in the sharply edged pool of light cast by the small antique lamp sitting on the table. Perry gave the marked-up draft to Todd and said, "I've made a few notes. Get the transcript from yesterday's hearing. I said some things that should be in here before Blauser collapsed.

"And I have a new task for you," added Perry, handing him a list of street addresses. "One of my clients is considering whether to acquire a privately held company called Thorn and Texas. We are illuminating the target's assets as best we can, from a search of public reports of its activities. I want you to make sure these properties exist and determine whether they're encumbered. Site visits first, starting tomorrow morning. Do not make a copy of this list and do not discuss it with anyone. You'll go with an attorney for the banker my client's engaged. The client will have a car here at 7:00," which left Todd exactly eight hours and 14 minutes to get home, decide whether to eat, undress, sleep (assuming he down-wired enough to sleep), rise up, shower, shave, dress, decide *again* whether to eat, and get to Danville's offices, because two minutes and four seconds had elapsed from the moment he entered Perry's office to the moment he left it.

For those two minutes of who, what, when, where, why, and how, Danville & Williamston billed the client $130.00. That was the weighted result of adding together Perry ($600/hour) and Todd ($180/hour) for one standard ten-minute billing-unit block of D&W time. There would be no charge to the client for the sheet of paper on which the asset list appeared because the client supplied it.

Yikes!, thought Todd in the cab that took him home. We shot right past *that* little courtroom drama, which he'd witnessed with his mouth hanging open. When Blauser fainted, Perry kneeled down beside him, loosened his collar, pressed an ear to Blauser's chest, and stepped away without a second look when the doctor charged up out of the audience to lend a hand.

And speaking of going rates, Todd revised his recommendation on Todd Brooks common stock in the *very* volatile D&W associates market: "sell" became "hold," because the sole shareholder in Todd Brooks common — Todd himself — had just got his first-ever need-to-know assignment. A provisional "hold," Todd cautioned himself, but a hold nevertheless. A state near to grace.

Just once, though, just for fucking *once*, could Stockbridge say "*Our* client"?

Ten

From the outside, the block-square, gray-granite City-County building appears to be one structure, but it has two hemispheres, like the human brain. There is a City hemisphere (west, on LaSalle, just up the block from Danville & Williamston) and a County hemisphere (east, along Clark Street).

The right-brain/left-brain assignments can change with administrations. The Mayor and the President of the County Board of Commissioners are never the same person even when the two governments work as one, because a meat puppet holds one office at the behest of the puppeteer in the other.

It is possible to walk directly from the City side to the County side on only four floors of the building: Floors One, Five, Seven and Ten, three of which are prime numbers. To help John Q. Public reach his destination, on Floor Number One in the west corridor, there are City office directories and banks of elevators; in the east corridor, there are County office directories and banks of elevators, and they look different. If John Q. wants to go to one of the floors where there is a wall, an actual wall, between the two governments, but he ignores the directories and gets on and off the wrong bank of elevators (as Milton did), he has to walk up or down one or more flights of stairs to reach his destination.

But Milton didn't mind the exercise, not a bit. When he finally, aerobically, reached the treasurer's office, he took a number, a seat, and deep, slow breaths while he waited patiently for service, which he received from a very pregnant 24-year-old *latina* named Gladys Rodriguez.

Milton handed Gladys the notice he had received and explained why he was there. Gladys touched a few keys and pulled the auction information up on her screen. "The taxes were paid by a land trust. Land Trust 14178."

Milton asked, "Who owns the trust?"

"Oh, I cannot tell you that," she said, apologetically. "I don't know." Gladys explained that Illinois permitted land ownership through trusts where the identity of the real owner was legally kept a secret, and it *is* hard to imagine a more efficient way to stump the posse, isn't it?

A dim memory confirmed this and prompted Milton to ask,

slowly, "Who is the ... trustee?" and smile, because he'd dusted off his nomenclature and gotten it right the first time.

"A bank," Gladys replied, dimpling a bit herself. "First Standard Guaranty of America." She wrote down for him the name of the bank and its address, a post office box-number.

Milton thanked her and left, wondering (1) how he was going to find out who wanted his building and for what purpose, and (2) whether Gladys would have a boy or a girl, or maybe twins or — crikies! — triplets.

Eleven

Fortified by a blueberry danish with enough sugar to cause his fillings to vibrate, self-esteem roller-coasting all *over* the fun park between his ears, Todd ducked into the car supplied by the client and found himself next to Louise Melville. She was severely turned out in charcoal gray jacket and skirt, eggshell blouse, and black flats. "Hi-hello-how-are-you-fine-me-too-what-a-surprise" completed, Todd said, "I thought you were with Westlake and Thomas."

"I was, but I moved to Heller and Pratchett." Louise smiled. "I couldn't resist a twenty-two percent raise."

"Spare me, okay?" Todd settled back sulkily in his seat and remembered Mark's successful ploy of the other night. He bookmarked it for a later retaliatory insult and asked where she wanted to start.

"How about starting southeast and working our way northwest?"

He shrugged. "Fine, whatever."

For the next seven hours, they drove all over Chicago. They stopped to stand in front of, walk around, and through, "component distribution centers," formerly known as 'warehouses," "low-rise shopping plazas w/drive-up-curbside-angle-parking," also known as "strip malls," and "high-rise residential towers," which used to be called "apartment houses."

Enough. It suffices to report here that they saw many big buildings, old and new, where people did a lot of different things, or where nobody did anything, because there was nobody and nothing there, except four walls and a roof, plus or minus plumbing and wiring.

The weather was balmy, and it was pleasant to be away from their plantations. They stopped for lunch in Little Italy, chewing Al's Italian Beefs with sweet peppers and slurping Mario's Italian ices on the sidewalk of Taylor Street.

By mid-afternoon, Todd and Louise had rocketed right past "civil" on the relationship meter and were asymptotically approaching "cordial."

At 3:18 p.m., they stood in front of Listing 17. Todd stared up at it, perplexed, and said, "This can't be right." Listing 17 was, well, *actually* listing, a small two-story red-brick building, leaning hard over the eastern two feet of the vacant lot to the west, as if it longed only to fall and forfeit its scruffy sham solidity once and forever.

Louise stood beside him on the sidewalk. "What a dump, to quote Ms. Davis."

Todd said, "It is a dump. Good thing we're not supposed to confirm valuation."

They walked around the building, warily. Todd anxiously scanned the block for hostiles, finger poised over the "Flight" button on his "Fight or Flight?" internal instrument panel. He wanted to leave that place before anyone took note of their demographics and decided to carve off a slice of their net worth. "Well, it's here," he said. He touched her arm, adding, "Let's go."

Louise lingered. "Is it abandoned?" She pushed the buzzer, looked for mail labels on the front door. Nobody answered, and there weren't any. She pushed open the front door, and peered up the darkened stairway. "Oh, ick." Louise backed out of the doorway quickly, retreated to the car.

Todd, however, was unaccountably ignoring his recent urge to flee. He stood staring up at the building, hair on his neck bristling. He moved toward the doorway, jerked closer by the bang and slap of one fact against another.

Fact Number One: Perry gave him the list of properties on which appeared Listing 17.

Fact Number Two: so far, every property but Listing 17 had been large, and investment-grade.

Tumblers in his skull clicked smoothly, silently, into line with another. Something, Todd grasped, is ... *different* here. Listing 17 does not *belong*. Listing 17 is an *outlier*.

Impelled by the tectonic friction of these ideational plates, a super-heated syllogism bubbled up through the crust on his consciousness, cooling and hardening into "if ... " and "if ... " and "then ... "

Far above this igneous process, backlit on comfortable couches in an Olympian Green Room, sipping expensive bottled water, no carbonation, please, sat ... who? The Gods of the Circuit? And were they *smirking*, their halos tipped back for casual comfort?

Todd pushed the door open and moved to the foot of the stairs.

The walls abutting the staircase were algal-green up to about three feet and then brain-gray to the ceiling. Paint peeled everywhere.

Todd gripped the staircase railing, ignoring the crud barnacling it. He began to climb the staircase slowly, watching his feet, placing each one carefully on a step and testing it before he put weight on it. He heard, or imagined he could hear, rustling and dripping in the walls.

Todd reached the top landing and stared at the door in front of him, rusty Master padlock secured against the barbarians at the gate. On the frosted glass, in intermittent gilt-edged, black letters peeling as enthusiastically as the paint on the walls, Todd read this:

Mil on B au e

And below, he read this:

t orney an Counse

The lines and planes of Todd's universe sighed and shifted, some acquiring definition, others forfeiting it. Figure became ground, and ground became figure.

Todd had read and heard of moments like these and always had dearly wanted one, but caution was wanted here, *lawyerly* caution. Facts must be gathered, Todd adjured himself. Many more facts, sorted, examined, ap*prec*iated, from all pertinent angles.

Todd felt an urge to shout and laugh, but it was too soon for that.

Oh, *much* too soon.

He turned to walk down the stairs, but stopped again, turned back. He read the sign on the door again, then a third time, tried to memorize every feature of the door, the frame around it, the wall around the frame. He looked for small defining features in the door, the frame, the walls, cracks or stains shaped in memorable forms, anything he could use later to put meat on the bones.

He walked slowly down the stairs and out to the car. As they drove off, Todd looked out through the rear window at Listing 17, smiling and silently *au revoir*ing.

Listing 17: 1138 West Madison.

Blind pig gets acorn, thought Todd. Stop the presses.

Twelve

Location, location, location.

Even if location is everything, a post office box is still the nearest place to no place at all. Unlike Oakland, California, a post office box has a there there, but it's a barely-there, a there mashed wet and flat against the underside of the non-skid safety cap on the leg below the lowest rung of the evolutionary ladder of theres.

A post office box has location, *is* location, but the there of a post office box is not the there of the post office box-holder, an object with location *and* velocity that cannot be measured simultaneously.

Milton needed a box filled with objects like him, objects that had location and velocity.

This essential difference between post office boxes and real addresses mattered to Milton, because he had and wanted one of each. Unlike his post office box, 1138 West Madison had Milton in it, the option package that transforms a location into a *place,* an address with an *identity.* And, *and,* Milton possessed location and velocity that were a product of all the locations and velocities of all the hits, near-hits, and misses-by-a-country-mile of every object that preceded him.

This head-on un-helmeted collision of uncertainty and determinism irreparably rent for Milton the illusion of free will, but it enabled him to deploy primitive information technology assets, once he remembered what phone books were and where they were. When Milton put his hands on one, he blazed a trail straight and true through the "Firsts," and the "First Standards" and even the "First Standard Guarantys." The "of" threw him at first, but he puzzled it out, leapt over that prepositional tiger-stake pit.

And found First Standard Guaranty of America.

Sixteen FSGA offices, scattered across the city and near suburbs. Sixteen boxes with *addresses. Evolved* boxes, with oak doors and parquet floors and replicas of the big old wood-framed clock with wrought-iron hands and roman numerals that hung in the original First office hanging over third-world ceramic planters, and peach walls covered with soothing prints of country-scapes by early Impressionists and bullet-proof picture windows and time-lock vaults and silent alarms and money that exploded paint all over desperate small-time robbers and free-standing counters with built-in lamps and waste-paper slots and leashed pens and glass-topped pigeonholes for transaction tickets and large bristly brown mats inside the front doors in winter and little yellow flat plastic silhouettes of men with hardhats standing guard next to them, warning you about wet spots on the floors. Boxes filled with security guards and cubicled loan officers, assistant vice-presidents and affirmative-action managers. Boxes with automatic telling machines and non-automatic-non-machine *tellers*, tellers of tales and paper trails, telling him, telling *to* him, who wanted his building.

"Location and velocity," he repeated softly, as he wrote each FSGA address and trust department phone number on the back of a page of the deposition of a long-dead witness from a long-lost case.

Get off this, get past this, thought Milton. Get in a box with *people* inside it, not a box inside which people merely reached.

He ran his pay-phone bill to $3.85 before he got in the right box, the branch that held the trust that bid on the tax deficiency that liened and leaned on the building that Milton owned.

Thirteen

The Thorn and Texas property analysis report in his lap, Todd flipped impatiently through it to the section for Listing 17. He read *this*:

Property Address: 1138 West Madison, Chicago, Cook County, Illinois, 60607.

Description: Two story, brick, w/ storefront (Fl.1) and office (Fl.2). Square footage: 2440/floor.

Lot size: 25x125.

Vintage: 1892 (approx.).

Permanent Real Estate Index Number: 14-07-204-021-0000.

Volume: 475.

Owner of record: Blauser, Milton Armitage (indiv.).

Fee: Simple.

Mortgagee: None.

Taxes: Delinquent (del. amt. = $9,418.00). Tax deficiency bid by land trust, owner/beneficiary unident. Redemption period pending; expiration date 07-29-04.

Liens and encumbrances: See "Taxes," above.

Other data: None.

Investigation continues.

"Well," thought Todd, swiveling in his chair, well-well-welling and oh-reallying and my-my-mying once each, for good measure.

But silently, because Perry forbade his associates to talk to anyone about their work. Even themselves.

Todd typed these three lines on his screen:

Land Trust<-->1138<-->Blauser

Client<-->1138<-->Blauser

Acquiror <=??=> Land Trust

Because his job depended on his getting it right the first time and every time, Todd always listened to Perry very carefully. Todd recalled Perry's handing him the list, describing it. So, Todd added a fourth line:

"asset inventory" <=??=> "these properties"

"Aaach," muttered Todd. These observations were inchoate; they did not fucking *mesh*. Todd added more lines. These were paired names:

C. Ahab/M. Dick

Holmes/Moriarty

Javert/Valjean

Stockbridge?/Blauser

And two questions:

What works? What sticks?

Todd yawned and rubbed his eyes. It occurred to him that he had $149,038.14 in his money-market account and an itch to put it in play.

He exited this private file, causing the computer in Perry's office to chime, twice. "These are the *firm's* offices and equipment," Perry warned each new hire, "and they are *never* to be used for personal matters. They are here for the clients. Unauthorized uses are theft of the firm's assets."

Perry had employed a byte-wise ex-spook from the National Security Agency, the federal hall of mirrors, to install an undetectably encrypted one-way observational overlay on The Kennel's networked computers. The lapsed spook approved Perry's choice of the chimes from the menu of activity-signals. Chimes for the doors of perception? Just the *right* accent, really. And she'd called Perry that day, inquiring about prospects for additional assignments, declaring herself ready, willing, and able as always to exploit misplaced, unreasonable expectations of privacy, here, there, and everywhere.

To Todd's credit, he got the names right, but — oh, imperfect Todd! — he got the order wrong. From his lower left desk drawer, which was otherwise always locked, Perry extracted a manila envelope. From that, he withdrew a faded sheet of stationery, traced with his right index finger raised black letters on cream, announcing the association and location of Stockbridge & Blauser, Attorneys and, yes, Counselors.

For Todd's questions, here are Perry's answers:

1. The struggle between good and evil.

2. The struggle to distinguish good from evil.

Fourteen

On the first ozone-alert Saturday morning in July, Milton found in his post office box an attempted-delivery note that directed him to the counter. The counterman handed him a package — a small box really — from the Attorney Registration and Disciplinary Commission of the Supreme Court of Illinois.

The Supremes run the advocates industry in Illinois. Through their diligent and discreet staff of accountants, investigators and — surprise! — lawyers, the seven Justices accept attorneys' annual dues, confidentially investigate complaints, and, after notice and opportunity to be heard, mete out exoneration or punishment for wrongs real or imagined but sufficiently proved.

The state legislature of Illinois, the "General Assembly," which is stuffed to its bilious gills with still more lawyers, *hates* the Supreme Court's hegemony over the legal profession. The legislators haven't figured out how to break the Court's fiercely defended bear-hug on their livelihood. Every so often, the Solons pass a law that purports to wrest the regulation of lawyers from the Court. But, at the behest of some convenient and friendly plaintiff who doubtless hopes to sit on the Court one day, the Justices speedily declare the law an unconstitutional trespass on their power.

The legislators can't get hold of even a *fistful* of their goddamn dues, which just shows, as between these two constitutional branches of government, which has the better lawyers.

Oblivious to this fandango of frustrated sausage-making, Milton opened the box from the A.R.D.C. He found, not a complimentary chafing dish or a fruitcake, but a letter. No, wait, there were two letters, one short and one long, on a stack of documents four inches thick.

"Dear Mr. Baluser," said the short letter from a discreet A.R.D.C. lawyer who wasn't, however, a diligent proofreader, "the Commission has received a complaint concerning your professional conduct. Attached is a copy of the letter of complaint and other materials provided by the complainant.

"To assist the Commission in determining whether to commence a formal investigation," the A.R.D.C. boilerplate continued, "you are invited to reply by letter, within 30 days. You may attach whatever documentation you deem appropriate for consideration by the Commission. There is no requirement that you reply to the letter of complaint, but the Commission may find your response helpful."

The A.R.D.C. letter closed with the phone number of its author, whom Milton was advised to contact if he wanted more information. Notably — pointedly — Milton's A.R.D.C. correspondent omitted best wishes to Milton.

The long letter was a photocopy of Perry Stockbridge's relentlessly negative screed on Milton's competence and diligence in their recently concluded lawsuit. Without explicitly imputing murderous intent to Milton, Stockbridge's letter conveyed an unmistakable impression that Milton harbored the motive and means to cast the entire Illinois legal system into the lightless hell of anarchy. The letter closed with a request that Milton be shorn of his license.

The A.R.D.C. letter was dated one day later than the Stockbridge letter. D&W letterhead had unique cachet at the Commission. One of the Supremes had practiced at each place for a time as a young lass. Taking note of the dignified, regretful tone of the letter, and the painstaking three-pound appendix detailing Blauser's lawsuit's herky-jerky progress and regress, with all pleadings and hearing transcripts attached, the A.R.D.C. General Counsel growled, "Someone cared enough to send the very best. A prompt and thorough inquiry *damn* well better ensue!"

To the General Counsel, the Blauser complaint presented a welcome contrast to the correspondence in which the Commission usually trafficked: semi-literate, semi-legible squallings on both sides of wide-ruled, torn-cornered loose-leaf paper from immigrant-clients gulled by promises of undelivered and undeliverable green cards; incendiary bank statements launched by jilted secretary-bookkeeper-spouses, minutely identifying the numbered accounts and exact amounts of commingled client funds dissipated off-shore on exorbitantly priced fruit drinks for bimbos and himbos.

Todd Brooks would have been pleased to know the General Counsel's views. The assembly of his letter-bomb on Blauser cost

Todd the better part, indeed, *all* parts, of one week of workdays and frantic worknights.

To Milton, however, Stockbridge's complaint painted a rather confusing portrait *of* Milton. Was he a sorry incompetent or a diabolical syndicalist? Could he be ... both?

In the litigious waltz of western civilization, Milton had danced the successful lawyer's part for a time, a *long* time, a long time ago. He'd never actually created or destroyed anything then, other than the odd intangible "right" or "duty." In most matters, wing'd victory was nothing bad happening to his clients, or to his lunch in the partners' dining room, while his cash flow widened and deepened. But Milton's memories of his conduct in those days, those days that had gone by, were thinning out, twisting Moebius eddies on a soft summer breeze.

Shrugging, then stuffing the letters into his shiny yellow satchel, Milton tucked the box under his arm and waddled out of the post office. That morning, his destination was the intersection of Pulaski and Foster on the Northwest Side. On the southeast corner of the intersection, First Standard Guaranty had the branch that had the trust.

To get there, Milton rode the #8 Halsted Street bus north from Madison to Lincoln and Fullerton (3 miles), the #11 Lincoln Avenue bus north-northwest to Foster (4.5 miles), and the #92 Foster Avenue bus west to Pulaski (2.25 miles). This took 113 minutes, 41 of which elapsed while Milton waited at each bus stop along his route, like a stolid Muscovite in a Soviet bread line, for busses that always and only arrived in herds of three or more. When he had a seat, he rested his A.R.D.C. package in his lap, and his satchel on top of that.

First Standard Guaranty's branch at Foster and Pulaski was a small green trailer adjacent to a large black hole in the ground, the site of a promised mall that would rise in a year, anchored — but also lifted up — by a poured-concrete temple to FSGA's Corporate Mission Statement: "Quality is Vision."

Milton climbed the astro-turfed steps into the trailer. A neatly dressed young man in shirt sleeves sat at the only desk in the trailer, behind a potted cactus and nameplate that identified him as Gert Heisenberg, Personal Banker. On one side of his desk, at

Gert's left hand, was a single four-drawer, letter-width gray file cabinet; on the other side slouched Gert's right-hand man, a myopic uniformed security guard secreting boredom from every pore. Crutches leaning against the wall behind him, Gert eyed Milton and extended his hand. "I'm sorry. I can't come all the way up," he said, half-standing, half-sitting, half-waving in the direction of his crutches. "How can I help you?"

Milton put down his satchel and package, shook Heisenberg's hand and said at the same time, "You have a trust here." *Damn*, thought Milton, releasing Heisenberg's hand, not right, not right, start over. Milton started again. "You're the ... trustee ... for a land trust. The bank is. Land trust 14178." He held a finger to his lips. "Shhhh. It's a secret. The trust."

Heisenberg settled himself in his chair, uneasily leaking a sidelong glance at the security guard. He said, "And ... ?"

"How do I find out who the trust is?"

"'Who the trust is' ... ?"

"The owner of the trust. You know." Milton thought hard. "The ... the beneficiary. Come on. In the file cabinet over there." Heisenberg shook his head. Milton wondered why the young man couldn't stand up all the way. Had he lost his pants? Was that it?

Milton focused again when the young man said, " ... lawyers."

Fearing the worst from any sentence that ended with "lawyers," Milton said "What?" and the young man replied, "I said, I can't show you any files. You have to talk to our lawyers." The security guard straightened up, crossed his arms, and narrowed his eyes, aggravating his myopia.

"Ah," Milton nodded, "the lawyers. Of course." He had taken three busses to hear what he could have learned in one phone call. He needed to manage his time and motion more efficiently. He looked intently around the room and then stared across the desk at the young man. "I don't see them. Where are they?"

Relieved to chance on an exit from this dialogue, but planning to use one of his crutches as a weapon if he had to defend himself suddenly from a physical attack, Gert Heisenberg quickly opened his office directory. "Our law department, let's see," he said, and in a trice he found a name and phone number. He wrote them on one of his business cards for Milton.

Milton thanked him and turned to leave. "Wait," said young Mr. Heisenberg, reluctantly. Milton turned around again. "I have to ask if you want to open an account. Or buy stock. And give you literature."

"Why?"

"They know how many people come in." Heisenberg looked at the security guard, who opened the palm of his off-gun hand, revealing a manual people counter-clicker.

Pulling at his jaw like Spiro, Milton said hmmm, an account, well, hmmm, he'd have to think about it.

Gert handed Milton FSGA's account brochures and a copy of the latest annual report. Milton took them and left, leaving Heisenberg and the security guard squirming in the backwash from their short-lived adrenaline rush.

Business Marketing hadn't taught Heisenberg how to deal with fucking filberts, which reminded him that he was glad he'd majored in Finance. He couldn't *wait* to get the hell out of retail and over to the investment side. He was *ready*. He owned five pairs of suspenders and subscribed to two cigar magazines.

Milton read all the brochures and the annual report on the Foster Avenue bus on the way east to Lincoln Avenue. As he got off to transfer to the Lincoln Avenue bus, he dropped the brochures in a waste basket.

He kept the annual report though, because on the third page, he found a grip-and-grin photograph of the FSGA Chairman at the annual stockholders' meeting, a-grinning and a-gripping the hand of Perry Stockbridge, identified in the caption as general counsel to FSGA.

One plus one equals one, thought Milton. A.R.D.C. plus FSGA equals Perry Stockbridge. "Okay," Milton said very quietly to himself, "okay. And D&W. *Three* acronyms. My license and my building. Quality is Vision."

The #11 bus hurdled the potholes of Lincoln Avenue, rattling Milton's guts and spine and filling his nostrils with the stink of diesel fuel. He tightly hugged his yellow satchel and his box.

Fifteen

Early in their professional relationship, Perry's personal spook-in-waiting advised Perry to eschew his office intercom because it was "Insecure, sir. You know, penetrable?" so his secretary, Mary Margaret Carmody, had to knock and enter his office each time she took a phone call on Perry's public, unscrambled line. "Mr. Blauser is holding," she said.

Perry picked up the phone. The clatter of the kitchen at Athena's Arms overwhelmed Milton's voice.

"I can't hear you," Perry said loudly. "Say again."

" ... give up my license ... me keep my building!" shouted Milton.

Perry said, "I don't want your building."

"What!?"

"I don't want your building," Perry said quickly, tightly. "I want ... " Stockbridge picked through vengeance, justice, peace of mind, before he finished: "... I want to get on with things. Will you understand that?"

Perry white-knuckled the phone for a half-minute, trembling, listening to kitchen-Greek collide with kitchen-Spanish, waiting for Milton to reply. Milton did not speak again, though, and the polyglot polytonality of Athena's Arms' kitchen ceased suddenly.

Perry hung up then and turned his attention to the single-spaced, one-page memorandum squared up on his spotless, blotless blotter:

Privileged and Confidential
Memorandum

To: Perry Stockbridge
From: Todd Brooks
Re: Thorn and Texas's assets
Date: July 13, 2004

This memorandum provides a preliminary overview of the ownership status of the items identified as Thorn and Texas's asset inventory in Chicago.

Stockbridge remarked the "...the items identified as ..." and raised an eyebrow. Which meaning reposed in that phrase? Did Todd intend to convey rigorous, commendable skepticism, that he assumed *nothing* Thorn and Texas asserted was true until conclusively proven? Or was this Todd's first spasm of fatal *im*pertinence?

"Physical inspection of each item listed on the inventory confirmed their existence, locations, and superficial characteristics. Structural inspections and appraisals of the listed properties are scheduled."

Perry paused again, pondering the purpose of "listed."

"To date, the search has yielded, tentatively, only one anomaly. One of the alleged assets appears to be owned, not by Thorn and Texas, but by a Milton Blauser, in fee simple.

The property is subject to a tax lien. A land trust has bid successfully on the unpaid taxes, and the redemption period will expire in less than a month. The trustee for the unidentified beneficiary is a D&W client, First Standard Guaranty of America.

All other items on the list appear unquestionably to be assets of Thorn and Texas. The title company advises that it expects to complete its search not later than next Friday."

Perry asked Mrs. Carmody to tell Todd's secretary to tell Todd to draft a letter to Blauser on his sanctions motion. "Have not called or written to set a date," Perry dictated to his secretary. "Did not raise the subject when we spoke today. Respond or I'll seek additional relief. By day's end."

As she left, Perry considered the terror Todd would suffer trying to decipher which of Perry's phrases were text for the letter and which were Perry's instructions *about* the letter. That would serve the gutless asp for burying artless innuendo, *nuance*, in his memorandum, consciously or not.

Nuance is a Muse, thought Perry. She speaks through lawyers, impels their art, confounds their art, *is* their art. Oh, and their sport, too.

Perry strode out of his office and down the hall to reception. He rode an elevator down to the lobby. On a pay-phone, Perry dialed the number of the beeper his spook-manqué always carried. When the beeper chirped at him, Perry touch-toned the four-digit code that signaled his need for a meeting, an offer of work.

As Perry rode the elevator back upstairs, he reminded himself that *movement* is not *action*. Perry couldn't live with Nuance, but he couldn't live without her.

Sixteen

Detective Rollo Feinberg of the 12th District timed his progress through night law school so that he graduated one day after qualifying for his 31-year pension. With all paperwork signed, sealed, and delivered, he scheduled himself to retire in two weeks, spend a month canoeing the Boundary Waters with his beautiful twin teen-aged daughters, take the bar, and then sue the entire frigging Chicago Police Department chain of command right to and through the frigging Superintendent, for "failing and refusing, without cause," to promote him beyond detective because his name was Rollo. On his desk at home, on top of his pension and benefit forms, that's what his draft complaint said, right there in the second paragraph: "failing and refusing, without cause."

Other than their being, oh, anti-semitic *dick*heads, his name had to be the reason they denied him — a goddamn eagle scout of a cop — any number of rightful, well-earned promotions. His record was spotless and brimmed o'er with commendations. Over 31 years and 3 days, Detective Feinberg exhausted his patience and good will and propensity to suck ass to better himself, patiently explaining to ignorant partners — and the pricks up the chain — that his parents met in Belgium on the run from the Nazis, had admired Rollo May, that May was the late great existential psychologist, and oh, right, there was something called "existential psychology," that it *worked* for some people, all right? And that he'd vowed never to change his name right after he'd been beaten bloody by a sixth grader — another fucking kike no less — in the playground of their near West Side elementary school when the 11-year-old mockie bastard tried to make him bark and roll him — "Rollo! Rover! Roll over!" — in dog-shit, on his first day in the school after moving to the Near West Side of Chicago from 163rd and the Grand Concourse in the north Bronx, where a 10-year old named Rollo got a little *respect*, for Christ's sake.

In the 12th District station house on the southwest corner of Racine and Monroe, at 100 South Racine, Detective Feinberg scrolled through a list of forms on his terminal screen to "Complaint." He carefully pointed and clicked his mouse, as he'd been trained to do. The complaint form failed to appear and the prompt told him there was a hard drive failure.

Detective Feinberg pushed the screen away and said, "Shit."

Seated across the desk from him, Milton smiled sweetly and shook his head in sympathy. The detective rummaged around in his desk drawer for things to write with and on. Eventually, he found a stubby number 2 pencil and a pad of pink phone message slips. He tore one off, turned it over to the blank side, poised his pencil over it and said to Milton, "Name?"

"Milton Blauser."

Saving room for the meat of the complaint, Detective Feinberg wrote that down in the tiniest legible print. "Address?"

"1138 West Madison Street." Milton licked his lips, added, "Suite Two."

"Phone?" A tough question, it stopped Milton cold for a moment, but he said, "Temporarily out of service."

Feinberg snorted. "Like this machine, eh? Business or profession?"

Milton answered, "Busboy," adding "lawyer," after a breath's hesitation.

Feinberg nodded. "Immigration, OSHA?" Milton smiled sunnily, having not the slightest idea what the policeman was talking about.

"What was stolen?"

Thinking of his license and building, Milton said, "He's going to steal my ... " and Detective Feinberg — an excellent listener — held up his hand and said, "Whoa," so Milton stopped.

Faced with a hard drive failure and a fat little pasty-faced moron, Detective Feinberg asked, in a tone that sounded gentle but wasn't, wasn't, *wasn't*, "The robbery hasn't happened yet?"

Milton nodded. "Yes."

Detective Feinberg pinched and massaged the bridge of his nose, shook his head. "No."

Milton said, "No?"

Feinberg slumped back in his chair, picked up his mug of coffee that wasn't supposed to be cold, but was. He sipped it, grimaced, and said "Shit," again. In the general direction of Milton, he said, "Don't practice much criminal law, do you? No robbery, no crime. No crime, no complaint."

"Uh ... " said Milton. He thought. He smiled. "... Battery?"

"Who subjected you ... " asked Feinberg, adding for the benefit of the Criminal Law I God, and relishing the sudden memory of a crack-dealing, hooker-beating, un-seat-belted pimp he'd known catapulting terminally through the windshield of the pimp's gull-wing Mercedes, "... to an offensive touching?"

"Perry Stockbridge."

Feinberg sat up in his seat. "Say again?"

"Perry Stockbridge."

Detective Feinberg rested his elbow on his desk and his chin on his palm, and asked in the mildest of tones, "Is that right?"

Milton nodded his head vigorously.

"The lawyer? At Danville & Williamston?" The firm, the very firm, that declined to give Rollo Feinberg the courtesy of an interview when he'd applied for an associate's job, even though he was number-frigging-*two* in his class.

At Rollo's fifth-rate, *extremely* local law school, D&W interviewed only the top-grade students who also were on law review, "requiring, as I'm sure you understand, indicia of scholarship in addition to grades," said the letter signed by the recruiting director of the firm. D&W plainly didn't give a shit that Rollo was an *adult*, with a fully formed personality, a dedicated selfless wife who taught high-school English in a goddamn ghetto war-zone, and two beautiful teenaged daughters who were number one and number two in *their* high-school class but would not qualify for college scholarships because he and his wife — get this — made too much *money*.

Milton remembered, "I ... I was ... in court. He touched me."

"And you didn't consent?"

Milton shook his head.

Wanting body parts, Rollo asked, "Where?"

Rollo said, "In court. Federal Court. Last ... Thursday. Yes." Milton did not catch that Feinberg wanted anatomy, not geography, but Feinberg saw no point in pushing his point.

"Witnesses?"

"Judge Forrester. And her bailiff. Others in court that day."

Feinberg smiled and thought of his approved retirement and pension forms on his desk at home. "Well, Mr. Blauser. I'll get right on this." Rollo stood up and Milton followed. "I'll be in touch."

Back in his office, Milton muttered, "Doesn't want my building," while he searched a file in his office for unspent, hidden cash he might have missed in earlier inspections. "Wants my license. Wants me *homeless*." Perry's tactics felt to Milton like a c-clamp slowly tightening on his skull.

Milton found no money in the file, closed it, and wrote the word "Empty" on it, in blue crayon extracted from his yellow satchel.

Nowhere to run, nowhere to hide, but not dead yet. Self-defense, Milton thought, is every man's right.

Seventeen

But for the handful of tables occupied by early-bird diners too junior in their investment banking houses to graze up high on the *prix fixe* pasture, Mickey's was very quiet, because it was sixteen hundred hours naval on a beautiful Sunday. Next to his second double—bourbon—rocks-with-a-twist, Todd positioned a small cassette recorder at the middle of the table between him and Louise.

"This is voice-activated," Todd said. "Hello, hello, hello," he crooned into it. He looked up and across the table, at Louise. "Now you say something."

Louise crossed her legs, briefly exposing to Todd several hundred furlongs of drop-dead-black-silk-stockinged thigh. She raised an eyebrow and asked, "What if I don't want to?" smiling faintly, but indulgently.

"Okay," said Todd, pressing the stop, rewind, and play buttons, hearing both of them clearly, but minus first syllables, because the recorder did not start as quickly as they did. They sounded impaired, but he was satisfied.

Todd rewound the tape once more, swallowed a finger of bourbon. "This is Todd Brooks, speaking. It is 4 p.m. on Sunday, July 18, 2004 ... He pulled a square of white paper from his shirt pocket. Scanned it. Looked up at her. "I'm here with Louise Melville. Louise, please confirm your identity and state as follows: you agree that you will never repeat or use any of what I tell you in any of your own work without my prior express written permission. Okay? In any form?"

Calculating to the millimicron the shrift that Todd deserved, Louise said, "I'm going to treat those as rhetorical questions."

Todd only gazed at her, hands clasped between his knees.

"Todd, I ... " Louise sighed, "... oh, whatever. I won't use any of what you tell me ever without your express permission."

"Or repeat it. And prior express *written* permission."

"Fine. All of the above. I swear. I'll put it in an integrated writing. Can we move along? This is my afternoon off."

Todd thought for a moment, trying not to look below her chin, at any alluring part of her. "Okay," he asked then, "you read the Thorn and Texas analysis, right?"

Louise nodded, giving nothing away.

Todd said, "Remember that crappy little building we saw last week? It's not owned by Thorn and Texas. *Not* by Thorn and Texas. This guy owns it. A lawyer, a dead-bang loser named Blauser. Milton Blauser. Stockbridge just finished whipping Blauser's ass, and I mean, taking *re-bar* to it, in a truly goofy federal case last week. Perry wants sanctions now, and he's filed a complaint with the A.R.D.C.. He wants Blauser's license jerked."

Todd hunched forward in his chair. "Here's what else we know: Blauser's in default on his property taxes. A land trust, a secret land trust's bid on it, his little shack. *Blauser's* little shack.

"These are the things I can say. These are things we both know. *Public* things. Now, here are the questions. Why's Stockbridge aiming to obliterate Blauser? Who wants Blauser's tenement? And lest we forget, for the latter question, why?" Todd sucked bourbon, leaned back in his chair, and smirked at her.

Oh, god, thought Louise, he's reverted to type. Expect the least.

Todd asked, "Have I got the good facts here or what?"

Warily, Louise asked, "For ... ?"

Todd beamed. "A book. An *epic*. Raskolnikov and his conscience. The Furies and whoever the hell they hounded. An epic about *lawyers*. It'll make us rich. I'm in it, so I need you to write it."

"You're 'in it'? Meaning just exactly what?"

"Louise. I can't write this. I'm the guy who's going to track it to its lair."

"Track *what* to its lair?"

"The rest of the story about Blauser and Stockbridge."

"I'm sorry," Louise raised a hand to stop him. "I'm not going to say it, Todd. Not now or at any other point."

"Say what? *What?*" Todd was alarmed, fearing derailment of his dream.

"'You know, it's crazy, but it just might work.'"

Delighted, Todd slapped the table. "You're in? *Great!*"

"No I'm *not* in. I won't write anything for you.

"Listen, Louise, just give me one —"

"It's not mine, Todd. I'm not interested. I won't write it."

"Okay, okay. You won't be my Homer on this. I'll settle for

professional detachment. Please. I need to talk about this." He inhaled, then words spilled out of him. "I'm breaking new ground here. And I'm not going to violate any attorney-client privilege or engage in any unprofessional conduct." He added, anxiously, "I think. 'S'why I need you. A cool head. And hand." Shaking off memories of what that head and hand had done to him and for him in the past, he added, "A smart lawyer, a *consiglieri.*"

Louise said, "You think Perry Stockbridge is trying to destroy Blauser."

Todd nodded, not trusting himself to speak and scare off Louise as she nosed the baited hook.

"And you think there's a book in it." She smiled. "A best seller."

"Oh, *God*, I hope so!" burst out of Todd, in a rush. His eyes glowed. "The past, Louise. There's always a past. And I know this guy, this free-lancer. He retails lawyer gossip. A parasite's parasite. Who's in, who's out, who moved his practice group whence, thence. Which self-important little shit just made partner. He'll know. He's been at it for years."

"He'll know why Stockbridge wants to destroy Blauser?"

"Maybe." Todd paused, reconsidered. "Jesus, actually, I hope he doesn't. I have to get in first or it's all shit. I just want him to tell me if there's a history there. If there is, what it is." Todd held his hands up in front of his chest, about six inches apart, palms toward each other, fingers curved around an invisible, intangible sphere whose music he alone heard. "The idea is, I put it all together ... construct a great moral drama. Maybe a tragedy. Maybe just great trash ... ." Todd trailed off, smiled weakly, downed another half-inch of bourbon. "I don't know ... whatever. I'll take it. Whatever I can get."

He put his head in his hands and muttered, "Danville & Williamston's a fucking *rack.*" He looked up at her again. "Well, if you won't write it, will you help me keep my ass out of the sling? Cheer me on? Wear my letter sweater?"

Just then, Todd saw her as he hoped to God she'd been: thirteen years old, in an oversized navy-blue cardigan letter sweater, pleated ivory skirt, ankle socks and white tennis shoes, and pompons in her hands, smiling carelessly through her braces, a little black pony-tail bouncing on her freckled neck.

Louise interrupted Todd's heart-breaking contemplation of her lost innocence, and his. She stood up, asked him to order a bottle of mineral water. Todd stood up, too, unsteadily, palms on the edge of the table, challenging her: "Where the hell're you going?"

Louise considered counting to ten, which worked just as well for her as counting to ten, and said, "Where women always go in restaurants. Todd. Dial it down. Please. And order something to eat. If you get drunk, we won't discuss this more today, or any day. This isn't a game and it isn't a date."

In the iron embrace of desperate hope, Todd did as he was told. After dinner, over coffee and cigars, Todd looked at Louise and smiled. "I have to say something, Louise. I have to say ... 'Now here's my plan' ... " Then, Todd paused to suck in, savor, and release a small plume of smoke, ". . but I don't have one."

Eighteen

Sipping a Midlife Crisis — three ounces each of domestic spring water, foreign vodka, orange juice (*not* from concentrate), with a tablespoon of laxative fiber (smooth texture, *not* original texture), stirred, not shaken — Rollo Feinberg carefully weighed his wardrobe options for his field trip to Danville & Williamston.

In his closet hung outfits for all the special occasions of a detective's life: sweat suits; turtlenecks; short-sleeved sport shirts; and oxymoronic dress uniforms and designer jeans. Among these, yet royally set apart from them on its own rosewood hangar, hung his Interview Suit:; tailored for him and to him by the most conservative men's clothier in the Loop, it was navy-blue chalk-striped single-breasted natural-shouldered virgin wool, with two pairs of pants, *with* cuffs but *without* pleats.

Draping the suit jacket over his arms like a bolt of Persian silk in the *souk*, the salesman had warned Feinberg that the garment was *not* to be dry-cleaned more than once a year, no matter how often he wore it. "Dry-cleaning extracts the natural oils from the fabric, weakens the weave," the salesman had explained. "You *must* brush it, and you *may* press it," advised the salesman. So long as it passed the stink-and-stain test (*not* the salesman's words), Feinberg was exhorted to keep it the hell out of the hands of barbarian dry-cleaners.

Even as he wondered how many times the clothier's drummers cast these pearls of sartorial wisdom before swine like him, Feinberg was grateful, *relieved*, to receive the advice, since clothing stores terrified him into silence on even the threshold issues of fit and color coordination. The better the store, the more acute his panic. When he came home once too often in shirt-and-slacks combinations like a scoop of rainbow sherbet on a licorice cone, his wife forbade his shopping for himself. Never before had he even reached the care and feeding of garments.

Regardless, without telling her and after consulting career planning guidebooks and everyone he knew (except the fashion failures with whom he worked), he essayed the store himself, bought the suit himself, sunk — *himself* — an additional three hundred bucks into black wing-tips, a white button-down 100% supima cotton long-sleeved shirt (the only long-sleeved shirt he owned beside three flannel and four rugby numbers), silk tie, suspenders, and boxing shorts. The ensemble fit perfectly, especially the jacket, since the store's tailor, with grave but unspoken misgivings, had sized Rollo with his wallet, eye-glass case, badge case, shoulder holster, stenographer's notebook, and belt-loop handcuffs in or under the jacket.

Rollo felt good in his interview suit. *Powerful.*

He stuffed himself into it five times, for his "on-campus" interviews with the handful of large law firms that reluctantly consented to visit with night students at his law school, slumming because a rough might yield a diamond, or because a doddering elderly partner still caused enough rain to command, querulously, an unenthusiastic tugging of the hiring committee's forelock in the downward direction of the geezer's shabby *alma mater.*

After the interviews and the "Dear [Insert Name]" letters that followed them, Feinberg resigned himself to wearing the suit to his daughters' weddings and spilling champagne and wedding cake on it. He'd wear the thing to any grandson's bris, assuming boys issued, maybe leaving a piece of foreskin wrapped in a yarmulke in the jacket pocket until his wife, horrified, found it. And if he died after his spouse, he'd sit shivah for her in it.

Regardless of who died first, he planned to be buried in that suit, since he knew he'd never work for anyone in it.

So, to wring his money's worth out of the frigging threads, Detective Feinberg went to D&W dressed like he belonged there, dancing among the piranhas waiting for a cow to wade dumbly into their bend in the river of law. Freshly showered and shaved inside his interview suit, Rollo strode out of the elevator and into D&W's fiftieth floor reception area, into the brushed aluminum and dark mahogany.

And he felt *right.*

He hoped his eyes coldly measured the men and women in the reception area: clients waiting to be seen or heard by their lawyers or their adversaries' lawyers; frightened third-party deponents trying and failing to concentrate on the froth of a news magazine or the sedative of a business journal; bored, sexually ambiguous bicycle messengers encased in spandex and plastic knee and elbow armor, courier bags slung across their chests, helmets tilted down over their eyes nearly to their opal nose-studs. Secretaries, shirt-sleeved lawyers and law clerks scurried through the lobby.

After a glance or two in his direction, all of them, *all* of them, ignored him.

Jesus, thought Rollo, deflated, I'm just another prop on the set.

He locked his gaze on the D&W receptionist, who smiled conditionally at him. Her left foot hovered over her silent security alarm pedal; even the grayest of the gray mice who approached her might yank Uzis from under their coats and ventilate her and the firm's art collection.

Rollo smiled pleasantly, pulled his badge case from his pocket, flipped it open, and announced, in a clear, distinct voice, "I am Detective Rollo Feinberg from the Chicago Police Department. I'm investigating a complaint against Mr. Perry Stockbridge. This is his office, right?"

The receptionist blinked, asked doubtfully, "A complaint by Mr. Stockbridge?"

Thank you, honey, for not listening, thought Rollo.

Raising his voice slightly, he said, "No, ma'am. A complaint *against* Mr. Stockbridge. A *criminal* complaint. Someone," he added gravely, "has accused Mr. Stockbridge of committing a crime. The crime of battery." His peripheral vision informed him that passing employees of the firm had ceased sprinting through reception, and were instead strolling past, or finding the documents they carried so fascinating that they stopped outright to read them.

Lacking a plan for crowd dispersal, the receptionist asked if Mr. Stockbridge was expecting him. "Why, no," said Rollo, "I don't believe he is."

"I'll call his secretary. Would you like to have a seat?"

Rollo smiled. "Oh, thank you, no, ma'am. I'll just stand. I sit *way* too much for my own good. And my lord, all those *do*nuts. It's a wonder I can walk at all."

The receptionist scanned the firm directory, said, "I'll see if she's in," dialed a number, spoke softly into it, listened, hung up. "She's going to check his availability. She'll be out shortly."

"Is she now? Good, good." Trying to cop-swagger even as he stood at her desk shifting his weight from hip to hip, Rollo studiously avoided eye contact with anyone, aggravating the miasmal uneasiness pervading the reception area.

A small, neat bird-like woman with gray hair and large round glasses emerged from the interior of the firm. She looked at the receptionist, who nodded at Rollo. She walked over to him, and asked, "Mr. Feinberg?"

"De*tec*tive Feinberg. Yes."

"I'm Mrs. Carmody, Mr. Stockbridge's secretary. Will you come with me, please?"

She led him to a conference room with a three-sided view of the east, north and west, and said, "Mr. Stockbridge is in a meeting, but he should be out in five minutes. He asked if you'd be so kind as to wait?"

Expansive, loving his work, Rollo said, "Sure. No problem."

She offered him coffee, tea, water, juice or a soft drink. He asked for water, suppressing an urge to order a shot and a beer.

Mrs. Carmody left him. A young black woman wearing kitchen whites and a hairnet entered the conference room, carrying a silver salver. Upon it were bottled spring water (foreign), a glass, a crystal bowl of ice frozen from still more bottled spring water (domestic), a smaller crystal bowl of lemon and lime wedges, napkins, and a plate of freshly baked sugar cookies.

"Wow," said Rollo, and, "thanks." She smiled and left.

Rollo poured himself a glass of water but resisted the cookies, the devil's penny. He carried his glass to the window. Ignoring the still, small vertiginous voice in his head, he leaned against it, gazed down at the Loop, east across the Lake, and north to Waukegan. After he located the north branch of the Chicago River on the Northwest Side, he tried to find his tiny little house, a 22-foot square Georgian built in 1953, one of thousands cookie-cuttered throughout Chicagoland. His "starter home," in which he would start his decline to senility because he could afford nothing bigger or better.

Rollo recalled that it had been too small the day he and his wife had moved in, *before* their daughters had been born, before they acquired a dog and two cats. As he searched for his home, a soft voice behind him said, "My phone number here is listed in the public directory."

Startled out of memory, out of the delivery room in which he'd seen his daughters for the first time, Rollo Feinberg turned from the window to the door, to confront two men: Stockbridge and, next to him, a smaller, stocky man with curly brown hair, in white shirt sleeves and suspenders.

"Pardon?" asked Rollo, thinking, take no prisoners, Detective. *They* were merely lawyers. *Feinberg* was the *law*, in*car*nate.

Stockbridge said, "You didn't have to stage that vaudeville in reception. You could have called. This is a place of business. Many people earn their livelihood here, including," he turned his head to the man beside him, "Mr. Braidwood." Braidwood nodded. "Byron was in the U.S. Attorney's Office. He's one of my partners. I asked him along. I hope you don't mind."

"Oh, no, not at all," said Rollo.

"Hi," said Braidwood, a specialist in the defense of technically complex white collar crime that, stripped of regulatory filigree, amounted to theft from widows, orphans, shareholders, and taxpayers.

The three men shook hands by the head of the table and circled to opposite sides of it, missiles armed and radar locked on target.

Rollo waited for them to sit. They didn't, so he didn't. He put his glass down on the gray marble table top, pulled his notebook and a pen from a jacket pocket. "I'm investigating a complaint filed against you. Mind if I take notes?" Realizing he was being forced to write awkwardly while standing, Feinberg broadly eased a chair away from the table and sat in it. Stockbridge and Braidwood looked down at him, exchanged a glance, and sat across from him.

Perry said, "I don't recall committing any crimes lately."

I'll bet you don't, putz, thought Feinberg, but he said, "A Mr. Milton Blauser has accused you of battery."

Perry raised his eyebrows. "Blauser? When did I batter him?"

"*Allegedly* batter him," interjected Braidwood.

"Last Thursday, in a courtroom. You know anything about it?"

Stockbridge answered, "I'd like to talk to Mr. Braidwood for a minute."

"Sure." Rollo smiled, thinking, and what the fuck is *this*?

Stockbridge and Braidwood stood and walked to the other end

of the room. For several minutes, they went whisper, whisper, whisper to each other. Finally, Braidwood shrugged. The two lawyers walked back to stand opposite Feinberg.

Stockbridge said, "I think I know what this is all about. Mr. Blauser and I were in court on a matter. He fainted. I opened his collar and put my ear to his chest to check his heartbeat. As you must have observed," added Perry, "he still has one. Except for that, I didn't touch him, for any reason. Mr. Blauser is ... troubled. I have filed a complaint against him with the A.R.D.C. The Attorney Registration and ... "

Interrupting him, Rollo said, petulantly, "I know what the A.R. D.C. is." Rollo wrote, then looked at Stockbridge. "And that's it?"

Perry nodded.

"'Yes, that's it?'" asked Rollo pointedly, writing down his own words and looking up at Perry.

Abraded now, too, Perry said, "Yes. One of my associates was there. Todd Brooks. He can confirm this."

Rollo printed the witness's name with a flourish, closed his notebook and stood up. Without offering his hand to either lawyer, Feinberg said, "Thanks for your help. I'll be in touch."

Braidwood said, "What did the complainant say?"

"Enough," replied Rollo airily, turning his back forever to Braidwood. To Perry, Feinberg said, "You went to Holmes, didn't you? Night school, right?"

"Yes," said Perry, "I did."

"The placement office told me," said Feinberg. "I just finished there."

"Really? Well, congratulations. Will you take the bar?"

"You bet."

"Good luck. Since you successfully handled night school and your job, I'm sure you'll do well."

"And I'm sure you don't give a rat's ass," said Feinberg. Triumphal, or*gas*mic, he walked out of the room without looking back, adding two more portraits to his private gallery of dickheads, a collection more varied and numerous than the Art Institute's.

Nineteen

Perry's privacy consultant was, and intended always to be, an atheist among apostles of McCluhan, but only partly because subject and verb do not agree in the popular formulation of the dead man's creed. Media *are* media, and *message* is the message. Since her first day in her first career as an eighth-grade social studies teacher in Atlanta, Georgia, at 22 years of age, she rejected sloppy grammar and sloppy thinking on this subject and all others.

Preferring to create or collect data in lieu of hectoring mere children about them, she shortly quit teaching to join the Central Intelligence Agency. She left the Company for the National Security Agency, convinced that the NSA was more analytic and less politic. After caroming off the glass ceiling in the hall of mirrors, she moved on to establish her consultancy. On her own, she honed the skills she'd learned at the Agencies, broadened and deepened her experience in a variety of business opportunities, overt and covert, dry and wet.

When Perry decided his privacy wanted enhancing, he did not consult anyone he knew for referrals, and he did not use anyone who had any connection to him through his work. He found her midway through the Chicago phone book's listings for security services, under the eye-catching, allusive name of Langley Peach Privacy, Inc. Obliging him to use an assumed name and cumbersome codes, she permitted Perry to contact her references, who were silent or grudging or belligerently paranoid.

These responses were praise enough for him. He also appreciated that the oblique approach to references she required left no evident trail, no memory anywhere, that he ever considered or sought the services she offered.

Of course, having hired her, Perry could not but trust her. In for a penny, Perry reluctantly acknowledged, in for an irritating pound.

While sweeping Perry's office for listening devices on her first engagement for him, the Langley Peach mentioned that she could respond to messages in different media. For example, "Let's say a client gave me a photo with the name of its subject," she hypothecated in her soft southern accent, "why, I could collect and provide information about that person ... until I receive a red octagon."

"A stop sign," Perry responded, smiling. She pushed the dark hair hanging down over her left cheek behind her left ear and returned his smile. Perry felt an unaccountable stirring, and a conspiratorial chill he'd not experienced since the death of his wife.

The Peach continued: "Let's suppose a client sends me two photos? And they're identical but for the shading of the subject in one? I would understand that message to have two parts. Gather information and undertake surveillance."

"Because shading amounts to shadowing. How could you interpret," Perry asked, carefully, "a photo of a subject accompanied by a picture of a pair of scissors?"

"Why, I suppose I could understand it to ask me to cut the subject out of the picture. That'd be decommissioning."

"Would that be temporary or permanent?"

"Oh my," said the Peach, dimpling, "that question's unanswerable. In the absence of context."

Later, she added, "For that last message? Decommissioning? Unequivocal instructions are mandatory. One can't accept such undertakings without them. No one should suffer the consequences of an error in transmission, or cause anyone else to suffer them. Ever."

The Langley Peach kissed Perry on the tip of his nose and turned away. Pulling the covers up over her beautiful bare shoulders, she closed her eyes and fell instantly and dreamlessly asleep.

Remembering that moment, Perry asked Mrs. Carmody to send him the firm librarian, who knew how to get photographs of Blauser and Feinberg. He also asked her to bring in a copy of D&W's current Associates Directory. The directory contained a photograph of Todd. It did not present him in the best light, but no photograph had been taken yet of Todd, by anyone, for any purpose, in any good light.

Twenty

Clad in camouflage colors from his boots to his neck, Pontiac McDowell resembled nothing so much as a toad on stilts: bulging eyes under a low, receding forehead, pug nose, and gaping chinless mouth ran necklessly into his bulbous body on spindly legs. Depending on his blood-alcohol level, McDowell ascribed his Christian name to maternal admiration for the Indian chief or paternal love of his family's first car.

Upon graduating from journalism school in the year of the rock stars who choked on their vomit following the summer of love, and moved by the light-hearted spirit of offing the pigs everywhere, McDowell started *City Law*. His muck-raking law-trade tabloid led the cheering for struggling young lawyers embarked on a children's crusade for the poor and oppressed in America's legal underbelly.

Until *City Law*, legal newspapers were colorless, conservative enterprises, packed to their somber borders with daily dockets, practice notes, and photographs of lawyers stiffly handing each other plaques for spasms of public service. *City Law* thumbed its nose at the genre's self-serving conventions, exposed and mocked racism, sexism, and corruption among the overlords of bench and bar. McDowell also editorialized relentlessly in favor of heightened protection for the sacred guarantees of the Bill of Rights.

But Nixon's long knives pared away the funding for legal services, and Reagan's thugs mugged its mission. The white-hot flame of the civil-righteous guttered out in fatigue and frustration. Most of McDowell's readers cashed in their karma for the price of a passage to the safe harbor of conventional private practice.

Worse, they abandoned *Pontiac* along with their principles. *City Law*'s circulation plummeted.

Concussed by these dual hammer-blows to the movement for equal justice under law and his cash flow, McDowell transformed his tabloid. He reconfigured it to suit, no, to *pander* to, the new interests and aspirations of his audience. Ever so gradually, he trimmed his editorial policy to, and past, the vanishing point.

By its 30th birthday, *City Law* featured breezy trend-spotting columns on legal technology, marketing, and fashion from "practice consultants," the American aristocracy that an otherwise prescient DeTocqueville understandably missed; sycophantic interviews with managing partners of the city's largest law firms, extolling their enlightened corporate cultures and visionary business plans while hugging a rainbow of smiling associates and paralegals; lawyer-to-lawyer personal ads; and restaurant reviews ("4 scales of justice for ambiance, but only two for service, folks."). By McDowell's master creative stroke, he confounded, buried, *crushed* his competitors: he created *The Lawyer's Channel*, an instantly successful syndicated cable program that sorted out the New-Age relationship of the brawling, brutal urban market for modern legal services to pyramids, crystals, and Scorpio rising.

On his 53rd birthday (a propitious day for mergers and acquisitions, according to the *Channel*'s anchor-astrologist), McDowell sold *City Law* and *The Lawyer's Channel* to a Belgian media conglomerate for $19.3 million. He retained, however, the right and privilege to troll for legal gossip and purvey a column of his down-and-dirty morsels to a select list of publishers.

Some bloody day, McDowell hoped, his collected clippings would comprise the prosecution's case-in-chief for the mass guillotining of lawyers he foretold, *read*, in the greasy pieces of Cantonese sweet and sour pork swimming in scarlet sauce he chewed to mush each night in Chinatown, after his informants billed the day's last charges and staggered, cabbed, or drank themselves home.

McDowell agreed to meet Todd — one of his more fruitful sources — at the southwest corner of Wacker and Michigan Avenue at high noon. As they walked north across the bridge toward the up-market mall and brand-name exhibition hall Le Boul Mich had become, McDowell mopped his broad forehead with a camouflage bandanna. "Temperate?" he complained. "Fucking climatic zone's *any*thing but temperate. Six months ago, it was 10 below zero with a wind chill of 45 below. It's fucking 95 in the shade now. That's a 115 degree shift, and the fucking humidity's like 110! *In*fuckingtemperate, I say."

Because McDowell's work still appeared in media where his favorite four-letter word was out of bounds even in quotes from distraught victims of sensationally ugly malpractice, and because he craved at least *one* outlet for his frustrated anarchic impulses, he swore frequently and loudly, pitilessly publishing profanity when out and about. Adult suburbanites herding scrubbed small children into the vertical malls of Michigan Avenue turned in McDowell's wake to glare at him. Todd cringed; he pretended he was coincidentally beside, but not with, McDowell whenever the scribbler erupted in vulgarity more toxic than the unprocessed industrial effluvia leaching slowly through the brownfields under abandoned factories south and west of the Loop.

"You're a terrific argument for revoking the First Amendment," said Todd, who confined his potty-mouthings to private places and familiar faces.

Effortlessly crushing conventional syntax in his bare mouth, McDowell said, "We talk doesn't mean we share the same fucking vocabulary." McDowell switched subjects without putting on his turn signals as they passed between the City's two surviving newspapers; he reached down deep into his bag of legal gossip, and asked, rhetorically. "Why'd Stockbridge file a complaint on Blauser? Easy question. They were partners once. Not at first. Stockbridge is younger."

"Really?" asked Todd, on guard for impressionable minors in earshot, "He doesn't look it."

McDowell shouted, "So fucking what?" An approaching flock of elderly, chicken-necked, total-immersion Nebraskan Baptists crashed head-on into McDowell's obscene aural *tsunami*; they abruptly veered away and toward the curb. In disarray, they attempted to cross Michigan Avenue in the middle of overheating traffic forced to brake suddenly, drawing still more epithets in a hundred tongues from a United Nations of tourists in rental cars, steering with one hand and scanning their maps of the City for, yes, Michigan Avenue.

"The way I hear it, Stockbridge was bussing tables in some fucking country club and some rich broad, and I mean *fucking* rich ... "

"Of course you do," muttered Todd.

"... took a lust on him. Married him and sent him to law school, but only at night. At that shithole Holmes. I don't know what the fuck that was all about. She could've sent him anywhere, endowed a fucking chair or twelve without breaking a sweat.

"But while he was there, he got hooked up with Blauser. Clerking for him. Days. Maybe that's what it was all about, night school. She wanted his butt in gear from day one. Anyway, Blauser had this shitty-assed nowhere practice, this was in the early '60's, and rich bitch offered Blauser a little work if he took on Stockbridge after graduation. Some family shit, I don't know, and he did. And they fucking took *off*. Varrrrrooom!" McDowell sent a hand jetting off toward the leaden low sky.

"Stockbridge had a gift for rainmaking. The work poured in, a Mississippi of money. *Good* work, too. Stockbridge had this perfect fucking radar for deep-pocket winners and losers. Every fucking time, ring it up. And Blauser did it, all the work, because he had a talent all his own. Can we get a fucking drink or what?"

Todd said, "What?"

"Pay attention, laddie. Pay at*ten*tion. I'm fucking dying of thirst out here."

Peering into a future filling up with ... money? Todd said, "No, what was his talent? Blauser's? What'd he bring to the table? And then we'll get drinks."

Pontiac said, "He could do anything. *Anything.* Litigation, arbitration, mediation, negotiation. Put a legal problem in front of him, any fucking case, and he knew what to *do*. When to talk, when to walk. A smart bomb. Aim and fire. On his feet or in his pleadings. A federal judge wept, fucking *bawled* on the bench, during Blauser's closing argument for some robber baron. I saw it. I nearly puked right there in the fucking pew. I mean, Stockbridge was Blauser's fucking pimp and Blauser was Stockbridge's ... "

"Stop!" Todd cried out, anxiously remarking the approach of two nuns.

"Stop what? Why?"

"Let's ... stop here. And, and, get a *drink*," Todd improvised hastily. They were in front of a sidewalk espresso bar. "To go. So we can keep walking." Todd ordered iced coffee for himself and a lemonade for McDowell.

McDowell drained his lemonade in a single swallow. "So far as I know, Stockbridge never actually did any law. I'm not even sure he could, but he didn't have to. Just did face and handed off the work to Blauser.

"And they were a fucking cash machine. After a while, they got some other guys. After another while, Stockbridge had a kid by the bitch. The kid got popped for running his little red sports car into the only fucking oak on Oak Street with an ounce of coke I think in his lap. Before you knew it, boom, end of partnership."

"'Boom'?"

"Boom. Blauser was supposed to get the kid out on bond, but he didn't get there in time. The kid must have been shit out of his mind high because he snuffed himself in the tank. Passed out and swallowed his fucking tongue." McDowell grimaced. "Seizures or some such gruesome shit. Wifey copped a stroke. Stockbridge pulled the plug on the bitch and Blauser. Took the clients and the other guys and walked across LaSalle to Danville."

"Jesus!" breathed Todd, appalled and enraptured, doors blown off by this Big Bang: money, drugs, death, *the law*. And here in this tale was a *bonus* theme: revenge, in slow motion. One life and one career for two lives. And only Todd, only poker-faced-but-secretly-gleeful-Todd, had both halves of this treasure map, the past and the present.

"Now what do I get?" McDowell demanded, jerking Todd out of a fantasy about full-page ads in Sunday book supplements in *all* the major markets.

Momentarily shorted out, Todd stammered, "'G-get'?"

McDowell frowned and poked Todd in his chest. "Pay attention, Toddie," McDowell hissed, "This is my *calling*. My fucking *art*. Give me a stake I can *ram* through the hearts of the vampires. Speak, Toddie. Or I tell your boss you're sticking a finger up his tragic fucking past."

Todd smiled placatively. He briskly sketched a scoop on D&W's negotiations to acquire a bankruptcy-law boutique that had gorged itself to the point of bursting on the rotting corpses of failed S&Ls in Illinois.

Pontiac pronounced himself satisfied and Todd debt-free and allowed him to stroll away.

As he walked back over the river, Todd congratulated himself on giving no hint to McDowell of the story the journalist actually might kill to own. Infants like Pontiac, thought Todd, live completely in their heads. What to call it? Todd wondered. *An Eye for an Eye*? *Bad Blood*? No, no, not *legal* enough. *Summary Judgment*? Better. *Rough Justice*? Todd nodded happily to himself. That might work, yes.

He had enough title, Todd decided, but not enough story. Not enough *facts* to crank the fucking book. Or to get someone to write it for him, or with him. Todd smiled. Maybe McDowell'd ghost it. But it had to be *right*. He suddenly noticed that sweat had trickled down his lower spine and into his underwear. Some of his excitement trickled away, too, as he remembered Perry's summary plug-pulling in the case of an associate at D&W who once too often — twice, in fact — treated her lunch "hour" as if it were one.

In a picture window, a slim pale dark-haired woman observed Pontiac's reflection thoughtfully watching Todd's back, but not, not, *not*, in any sense that would have reassured Todd. From fifteen feet away, she did not hear Todd and Pontiac. Of course, she had positioned herself to view Pontiac's lips and read them, but, in the larger picture the Langley Peach was carefully developing, what he said did not matter.

Twenty-one

Milton emerged from the doorway of 1138 West Madison, stunned instantly by the broiling sunrise. At 6:22 in the morning, it was already 85 degrees. Asphalt fumes rose from temporary hot patches in Madison Street, shimmering and dissipating in the morning light.

Blauser carried his yellow satchel under his right arm. In his left hand, he clutched a small plastic supermarket bag filled with the debris of the past night's dinner and housekeeping, the handles tied into a neat bow to secure the garbage against spilling. His eyeballs packed in what felt like coarse-grained sandpaper, Milton wanted only to go to a cool place and put his head down and never raise it again, but only 17 days remained in the redemption period. Dropping the garbage bag in the first wastebasket he passed, Milton forced himself to walk the three blocks to the police station, where he hoped to find Detective Feinberg and receive a briefing on the status of his complaint.

Composed of sooty brick that was off-white, off-gray, off-cream, off-yellow, or just off, the two-story police station squatted on the north side of a small parking lot reserved for police vehicles. Milton enviously watched two smiling policewomen in work blues and bullet-proof vests climb into the air-conditioned cab of their squadrol.

At the intake counter, he asked to see Detective Feinberg. "He's out for a while," said the civilian desk clerk, "maybe twenty minutes. You can wait or leave a message."

Dizzily, Milton made his way to the hard wooden bench nearest the window air-conditioner. He sat, toes barely touching the floor. Dozed. Dreamed. On State Street, on a reviewing stand covered with bunting, the Cook County Treasurer accepted his check for $94 million and offered him the thanks of a grateful nation. Hydrants burst open all around the reviewing stand and drenched them. The Treasurer looked down at the check and she frowned.

Milton started awake, frightened all over again. "No fair," he whispered to his unconscious, "you're supposed to be on my side." He clasped his hands in his lap, kept his eyes on the station door, and did not fall asleep again.

According to the clock above the intake counter, of Milton's 17 remaining redemptive days, another 14 minutes passed, expired, drained away, went wherever the hell time goes, before Feinberg ambled back into the station, a brace of new canoe paddles cradled in his arms. When the detective saw Blauser, he smiled like the Treasurer in Milton's dream, a man about to leave an ugly life behind him, and pointed at Milton. "Blauser, right?"

"Yes." Milton nodded, brightened.

"Come on back." Milton followed Feinberg through the gray-green corridors of the station to the cubicle area he shared with the other detectives. Feinberg waved him into his cubicle, onto the cheap pine captain's chair beside his dented gray steel desk.

"Well," said the detective, "I saw Stockbridge. I got good news and bad news." Feinberg stopped and waited for Milton to take the cue, to say which news Milton wanted to hear first. Milton's silence, his complete disconnection from the shtick of everyday discourse, left Feinberg hanging until he realized he could go forward at will.

"Okay," Feinberg said briskly, "Stockbridge says you fainted and he was just trying to help. You know, loosen your collar, check under the hood. True?"

Milton thought. "Fainted, yes. But he touched me. *Touched* me. I didn't want him to."

Feinberg forged on, unperturbed. "I went to see the judge, too. Forrester. Federal Judges have nice chambers. Not like the criminal courts, 26th and California. Felony court. You probably never been there. A dump. The judge, well, she backed up Stockbridge. So did her clerk. And a wuss named Brooks." Rollo summed up regretfully: "I can't take this to the State's Attorney. Maybe you got a civil action, a tort, but I doubt it. He'll say he didn't *intend* an offensive touching," After genuflecting thus to the Tort God, the detective finished: "And I think he wins. He was trying to help, wasn't he? So that's it, Mr. Blauser. Good news for Stockbridge, bad news for you. Sorry." But it was fun, thought Rollo, rattling the bars of the cage, shaking up the dickheads, if only for a few minutes.

Milton blinked rapidly twice and said, "Can you give me nine thousand four hundred and three dollars?"

Feinberg frowned like the Treasurer in Milton's dream, mustered only a perplexed, "Say what?"

"I have fifteen dollars, but I need nine thousand four hundred and three. Nine thousand four hundred and three dollars *more*." Wanting no misunderstandings, Milton stated the account precisely. "To pay my taxes. Property taxes. Or Mr. Stockbridge takes my building. My *home*." He looked at Feinberg, tears welling in his eyes. "I don't have anyplace else."

Milton started to tell the detective about his building again, and this time, Feinberg, the excellent listener, did not stop him, did not send him away. As Feinberg read the balance sheet between them, he owed Milton a kindness. *One* kindness, not more, for leading Feinberg to Stockbridge, giving Feinberg the opportunity, the *cover*, to rattle the frigging bars. Due process for little Mr. Blauser, an unobstructed opportunity to be heard, Feinberg decided, was, well, due.

So Feinberg learned about Milton's building, the breakfast grill, the Health Department, the bookie and the mice, the bill from the Treasurer, Athena's Arms, the twenty dollars from Spiro, Milton's visit to the Treasurer's office, Gladys who looked like an imminent mother of triplets, the secret land trust, Milton's visit to the FSGA branch, the young man Heisenberg with the crutches who just might not have had his pants on, the picture of Perry in the FSGA annual report, the A.R.D.C. complaint, and Milton's call to Perry.

And as the finale, to get every last member of the cast up on stage for the big Hawaiian number, Milton pulled from his yellow plastic satchel the annual report of First Standard Guaranty of America. He opened it carefully to the dog-eared page where the FSGA president grinned and gripped Perry's hand, put the report in front of the detective, smoothed the pages. Milton put his finger on Perry's face and said grimly, "He *says* he doesn't want my building, he told me that, but the bank is going to take it." Milton sat back in his chair and folded his arms across his chest. "He's not going to stop it. Reading Feinberg's mind, Milton reiterated, "It *was* offensive."

Yikes, thought Feinberg, sound the lunatic-dwarf alarm, but, buying time to calm Blauser down, "Huh," was all he said.

"This is why I need nine thousand four hundred and three

dollars. Can you give it to me?" Glancing at the little clock radio next to the pictures of Feinberg's wife and daughters, Milton said, "That's another hour gone." He noticed the pictures, peered at them, smiled. "They're very pretty," Milton said. And, apropos of what, Feinberg was not sure, Milton muttered, "Self defense is my right."

Oh shit, thought Feinberg, tensing. He said, "Mr. Blauser, was that a threat?"

"A threat?"

"A threat. Against Stockbridge. Or my family."

"No," said Milton firmly, shaking his head, "Not a threat. *Not* a threat. *Never* a threat. I play by the rules. Follow the rules. *Win* by the rules. *Always.*"

Embarrassed by his suspicion, Feinberg told Milton, "I can't help. We're strapped. I'm sorry." And to his surprise, he was.

Milton stood up, picked up his satchel in his left hand. "I have to leave now. I have to go shower and work." He held out his hand to Rollo Feinberg.

With feelings more mixed than at any time since his daughters' admission to puberty, when he wanted to kill every boy who might ever speak to either of his beautiful children who wasn't a child any longer, Feinberg clasped Blauser's sweaty little paw in his own stubby-fingered, wide-palmed mitt and shook it. Among his mixed feelings was wonder, which Feinberg recognized when he urged, no, *implored*, Milton to visit again, "... anytime you're in the neighborhood."

Milton reminded him, "I live in the neighborhood," and left.

Alone and unexpectedly lonely, Feinberg bent over, grunting, and unlaced his shoes and parked his feet on a corner of his desk. Staring through the donut/police cartoons pinned to the fabric of his cubicle wall, Rollo drew up a mental list of everyone he knew who had $9,403.00 to burn, to flush down the frigging toilet on a loony busboy lawyer.

It was a short list, but it was a list, and Feinberg reached for the telephone.

Twenty-two

By turns, the aspiring writers' group binged on butterfat and purged with sprouts, so it met that night in Broken Idaho, a Wicker Park coffeehouse choreographed to dance the death of Nature.

Sipping cappuccino beneath black-and-white photographs of the Chernobyl hot zone and oil-slicked Arctic wildlife, Todd surveyed the room, amazed. Broken Idaho opened for, like, business, dude, only eight days before the group convened there, but it already met, no, *exceeded*, its quota of stock coffeehouse habitues.

Apparently, coffeehouse owners ordered them like potted ferns, from an alternative-culture mail-order operation on the high plain of South Dakota with an 800 number and overnight delivery. Broken Idaho got the blend of denizens just right: there were pale young *punkervolk* meeting and greeting, kitted out in black, black, black, freshly styled at Hair Hitler, the hot alternative salon in Wicker Park for off-the-shoulder tattoos, asymmetrically buzzed and colored hair, silver eyebrow rings and lip rods; work-booted, pony-tailed ersatz woodspersons in baggy khaki hiking shorts and olive-drab tee-shirts, earnestly filling page after page after unlined page of hard-cover journals with bittersweet memories of rejection by last week's lovers; and middle-aged suburban divorcees tucking into radicchio-and-feta salads, wide-eyed amid the middle-western warp and woof of politics, magic, music, muffins, and drugs.

Except for Louise, who was unusually late, the group sat cross-legged on throw-pillows, around a low table salvaged from a college-town pizza parlor, its legs sawn down to the one-foot mark. A hundred-thousand drunken undergraduates had carved into it their initials, stained it jet-brown with tomato sauce, olive oil, beer, and vomit.

Just before Mark began to read, Louise joined them, apologizing, and settled herself quickly on a cushion next to Todd. "Glad you made it," said Mark. Louise smiled at Mark, the master of seductive misdirection, and Todd reddened sullenly from the warmth in her smile.

Mark read his story about an eight-year-old boy's first trip to the Atlantic Ocean. Gnawing obsessively on Stockbridge and Blauser, Todd listened indifferently at first.

After a few minutes, though, the story caught Todd. With the rest of the group, he squeezed into the station wagon beside the boy and his mother and father and two younger sisters. Together, they all drove east from the coal country of western Pennsylvania. Driving through the tunnels of the Turnpike twisting among the Allegheny Mountains, slowing in a sudden downpour in high August, listening to the wipers click and rub. Across the Delaware Water Gap, turning south toward the pine barrens of New Jersey, all of them smelled and heard the ocean even before they saw it, or imagined they did.

That was where the story ended. The group sat silent for a moment. Ed breathed a "Wow," and JudyJudyJudy said in a small voice, "I liked it a lot."

Damian asked if the story was autobiographical. No, Mark said, he'd grown up by the ocean, couldn't remember a day in his childhood when it wasn't there. He'd driven east through Pennsylvania during college once, gotten lost in a rainstorm. That had happened, "but it's not about being lost," said Mark, happily baffled.

"I guess you didn't feel lost when you wrote it," said Ed.

Louise said, "Nothing's ever lost. Every time I lost a toy and cried about it, my mom took me in her lap and stroked my hair. She rocked me and said, 'Everything is in its rightful place, marked and held for its owner.'"

Lost innocence, thought Todd. Lost freedom. Lost self-respect. Lost dreams, careers, loves, lives. All piling up in storage. All tagged. If nothing is ever lost, Todd realized, he could find everything that was marked and held for him.

Further discussion of Mark's story wound down predictably to the editorial point of no return, where each part of the story worked perfectly for one listener and failed utterly for another. One by one, everyone paid and drifted out, except for Todd and Louise, who pretended to miss a hot wet hungry look from Mark.

Todd recounted the ballad of Stockbridge and Blauser as sung by Pontiac McDowell, minus the expletives. "That's it, then," said Louise.

Todd didn't answer immediately, suddenly wanting only the heat and weight and friction, the *release*, of Louise upon him, next to him, beneath him, all around him. But his hunger for a better story, no, a *complete* story, without any loose ends, momentarily routed his testosterone. He shook his head. "Uh-uh. Same questions, more questions. Why now? Why's Perry waited all these years? What's the goal?"

"More, more, more," teased Louise. "How Nineties of you. There may be less here than meets the eye, Tallulah." She yawned, looked at her watch, winced. "Oh, God, it's too early. I should go back to the office." Legs cramped from sitting on the floor, they rose stiffly, quit the coffeehouse, walked south along Clark Street in search of cabs. A hot wind from the south threw grit in their eyes, stirred up newspapers in the gutter, sent a plastic spring-water squeeze-bottle tumbling and clunking hollowly north along the street.

They spotted an empty cab, waved it down. Todd pulled off his glasses and polished them on his tie. "I was surprised tonight," said Todd, squinting down at his glasses, "by Mark's story. And by Mark," Todd added, surprised further by his burst of good will.

Louise smiled. "I was, too."

Todd held his glasses up to the street lamp, saw new smears on the lenses, put them back on, looked at Louise. "Are you actually going back to work?"

"Why?"

This time, Todd's hoping against all hope surprised him. "I don't know, maybe we can go somewhere," he suggested. "Maybe find something we lost."

Louise looked at him solemnly for a moment, then brushed the curve of his jaw with the tips of her fingers. "Let's try," she said.

Twenty-three

Rollo *knew* someone was watching him, following him. But he couldn't see his shadow, no matter how quickly he turned, and it was driving him *crazy*. He'd whirl around in the parking lot at the Racine Street station as he climbed into a car, or in the alley behind his home as he pitched the garbage into the cart. Wherever. Just beyond his peripheral vision, there always was movement that matched his, movement he *almost* saw again and again, but didn't see.

"Maybe you're fucking nuts," grunted Pontiac McDowell from the adjacent bar-stool. Coincidentally, McDowell popped into his mouth a palm-ful of *actual* nuts, of the beer-cashew species not found in nature.

McDowell and Feinberg for years had made themselves useful to each other, supplied information to each other. Feinberg never accepted money from McDowell when they talked, and McDowell never offered it. They just wanted to know what each knew about things that made their jobs, their *callings* — making cases and breaking stories — more, oh, *int*eresting. Pro*duc*tive.

They were reciprocal sources, symbiotic, tongue and groove, like cops and lawyers who manufactured accidents and victims and profited from them. They contrived to meet irregularly in rural Illinois, in roadhouses neither owned nor frequented by Chicago cops or journalists, where all the other customers, if there were any at all, drank in bib overalls or camouflage clothing or orange hunting suits, where McDowell looked local, unexceptional, unexceptionable.

Rollo motioned the bartender over. "I want another, you know, orange juice and vodka," he announced, "this time," pointing to the blender, "in there." "With ice. Throw in a banana if you got it." Out of his tee-shirt pocket, Rollo pulled a small plastic sandwich bag with powder and dropped it on the counter. "Put this in. A tablespoon."

The bartender — squarely muscular beneath bib overalls, a scraggly Van Dyke on an open and friendly face under a head of dirty-blond country-stoner hair — stared at the little bag apprehensively. "What is it?"

"Fiber."

"Fiber?"

"Fiber."

"What does it do?"

"What does *what* do?"

"The fiber."

"What does it do? It does what fiber does."

The bartender thought. "It helps you take a dump?"

"Eureka," said Rollo, dryly.

"Urethra!" mumbled Pontiac, sliding smoothly off his bar-stool and marching off to where women *and* men always go in bars.

As the blender whined, Rollo thought about his elusive shadow and Milton Blauser, his stumpy, obvious shadow. Rollo could get someone to watch his back. Hell, he could get someone to watch his front and sides and bald spot. He knew enough guys with time on their hands, retired guys who no longer worked off-duty security at concerts and ball games. The agencies preferred working cops anyway, who were always younger and usually crazier, and more intimidating.

Setting a pint glass filled with a frothy yellow shake in front of Rollo, the bartender asked, "What do you call it?"

"It doesn't have a name."

The bartender smiled so widely Rollo could count all four gaps where teeth belonged, three up, one down. "Well, how 'bout we call it a Vodka Flush? Or a Regular Russian?" Hooting through the toothless places, the bartender moved off to the other end of the bar.

"Age is a fucking indignity," grumbled Pontiac as he got back up on his stool. "Bladder's the size of a pinhead."

"You could get a, what is it, a catheter. And a little tank on wheels."

Pontiac glared at Rollo. "Pig."

Preoccupied, Rollo did not reply with his customary sucking, snuffling sound.

McDowell noticed. "So, what's new and different?"

"Don't you mean, 'What's *fucking* new and different?'?"

"No, I don't," sighed Pontiac, "I would have said that if I fucking meant that."

"And you always say what you mean."

"Yes, I do. Now, which is it? You a fucking source today or just a fucking drunk?"

"A source. An unimpeachable source." And Rollo told him about Blauser's complaint against Stockbridge, Rollo's trip to D&W, Blauser's story of his building, and Rollo's take on Blauser: "Harmless. A character, but *with* character, you know?" Rollo said hopefully, testing McDowell, probing him.

Well, here's a fucking *run* on Blauser and Stockbridge, thought Pontiac, a bull market in them. Input *and* output. And, here's Mr. fucking Brooks again. He didn't tell me this? This is much better than skim milk about D&W buying a bankruptcy practice. Retaliatory criminal complaints, secret land trusts. This is fucking *sweet*.

"... a favor, this time. Not information."

"What favor?" McDowell asked, suspiciously.

Rollo looked down at his drink, rotated it on its coaster, cannonballed on in to the pool. "This guy Blauser needs $9,403. I'm thinking you should give it to him."

"Give money to a fucking lawyer? *Me?*" McDowell's voice rose sharply. From the other end of the bar, the bartender, a little concerned about the decibel level from the amphibian in the camo suit, looked up from the latest issue of his guns-and-babes magazine.

In a soothing voice, Rollo, said, "Look, the guy'll be homeless."

"Mercy," said McDowell, wonder in his voice. "Absolutely not," he said, shaking his head, "No. Fucking. Way."

Falling back to his second line of argument, just as he'd learned to do in law school, Feinberg said, "Screwing Stockbridge'd be excellent. He's a dickhead."

"No. That's the same thing. You still got me giving money to a lawyer." McDowell had his decision rule, and he was sticking to it: No money to lawyers. "Ever. Uh-uh."

McDowell didn't use lawyers for *any* purpose, didn't even use them to sell his paper. Poking himself in the chest, he said, "I drafted the sale agreement. Me. The Belgies got the paper, and I got the right to keep writing whatever I wanted, whenever I wanted. And they didn't stop payment on the fucking check, so it all worked out fine. *Without* any fucking lawyers."

Third line of attack, thought Rollo. "Okay, I'll take it. Give the money to me. I'm not a lawyer." Yet, he added silently.

"And you give it to Blauser," McDowell accused.

"Mmmmm, maybe." Rollo smiled. "I won't tell you. Your conscience'll be clear. Come on, give a shit for once. You can afford it."

Tangentially, McDowell was solicitous: "Won't you get in trouble?"

Feinberg shrugged. "Nah, I don't see it. It's like if a guy came up to me and filed a report and said he was robbed. I could get up a collection for him right there in the station. Blauser's complaint is shit. Nobody'd take it to the State's Attorney."

McDowell threw some money on the bar — *not* $9,403 — climbed off his stool, said, "I'll think about it," and toad-stilted out of the bar. And he *did* think about it, and about a big fucking bank counseled by Perry Stockbridge taking Blauser's tenement on a nowhere block on the Near West Side. Letting that happen, mused McDowell, makes an even better story, yeah.

Twenty-four

In a windowless D&W situation room, papers concerning Perry's client's proposed acquisition of Thorn and Texas reposed in thirty-one stacks of varying height on a table as long and wide as a bowling lane. At the end of the table, next to one especially tall paper hillock, Perry and Todd stood with Simon Smythe, a title officer from Heartland Title and Trust.

Smythe shifted uncomfortably from foot to foot, like a small boy awaiting discipline in the principal's office. He was English, of the class of post-Imperial twits that repeatedly, unconsciously, and disagreeably scattered "ummm" and "uh," and "ah" throughout their syntax. Smythe asked Perry, "Do you own real estate, Mr. Stockbridge?"

"Yes."

"Ah. Good, good! And ummm, your tax bills, do your bills have your name on them? Or the name of the uh, the prior free-holder?"

"My name."

"But at first, for some period, did the bills, did they ummm, did they bear the name of the prior owner?"

"Yes."

"Exactly! And that is our little problem here." The title officer patted the hummock of documents next to him on the table. "Or rather, a part of it. Now, my staff have gone back in our little time machine to 1988, when Blauser bought the building. Mr. Blauser's building. From The widow Palazzolo. There is ummm, no *cloud* on that transaction. No." Smythe picked up a folder off the peak of the little hill and handed it to Perry, who handed it to Todd, beside him, without even glancing at it. "See for yourself," Smythe suggested to Perry then, pointlessly. "Your Mr. B. bought the building. Took title. Recorded the transaction with the Recorder of Deeds. Properly, cleanly," said Smythe, beaming, "*surgically*. But after that ... " the titleman trailed off, sadly shaking his head, then picked up the thread again, a thought beyond where he dropped it. "Government can be so slow, you see. Processing the ummm, uh, the paperwork. When there is a lot of it. We ummm, we don't know."

"Don't know ... ?" echoed Perry. A tingling brushed, touched, caressed, the ends of Todd's nerves.

"Ah. Don't know who, uh, who owns the building. Don't know if anyone does, actually. Hah. There have been a number of, uh, transactions, presented to the Recorder's office since then. Transfers. For recordation."

"How many?" Perry asked tightly.

"Ah. Well, we uh, we don't know that just yet. Give us a bit, though, a bit of time, and we'll sort it out. I don't doubt it."

Perry said, "Just exactly what do you know?"

"The uh, building seems to ummm, uh, seems to change hands rather frequently. And the land. Sometimes they go together, sometimes separately. For varying lengths of time. A day, a week, an hour, a month. Very irregular," Smythe lamented. "Back and forth. Around and about, I should say. Among Mr. Blauser and certain ummm, uh, corporations. Including T and T. Thorn and Texas. And partnerships."

"How many?" Todd heard, but did not *believe* he heard, urgency, *anxiety*, in Perry's voice.

The title officer plucked a list off the summit of another of the piles of transfer documents. "Ah. Here is a list," he noted unnecessarily. "Of transactions and ummm, uh, parties. It is only provisional." He handed it to Perry.

Perry scanned down the list, said harshly, "Thirty-one?"

"So far," the title officer said nervously. "We think that carries us into, ummm, uh, 1992."

Perry rolled the list into a tube and tapped his palm with it, working to calm himself. "When do you think you'll finish?"

"Well, we can't say just yet, sir. There is ummm, a backlog at the Recorder's office, of course. There always is. We don't know that the Recorder has found all of the transactions. And we don't know how many of them are genuine or, ummm, uh, shams. Could be all or none, or uh, some. Of course, it doesn't matter," said Smythe, cheerfully. "Ultimately. Because of the, uh, taxes. Redeemer's rights are superior to any owner, whoever it is, because redeemer pays the taxes. Pay the taxes, cut the, uh, the Gordian knot, I should say."

Milton knows that, thought Perry, even if he's forgotten everything else. "Get on with it," Perry said to Smythe, who replied, "Right, then," and saluted smartly, before he remembered he was plowing paper for a predator, not taking the helm of a Royal Navy cruiser in 20-foot swells on the North Atlantic.

As Todd and Perry strode out of the document room, Todd said to Perry, "This might explain why the building appears to be owned by both Thorn and Texas and Blauser."

Perry stopped, looked so closely at Todd that Brooks felt like a specimen mounted on a slide. Stockbridge said, "These relationships between Blauser's building and other entities. Do you understand them?"

"No."

"Understand them. Advise me about them." Perry handed Todd the list. "Thorn and Texas is on the list. Twice. Has that really happened? How many more times have they dealt with each other? To what end? With what result?"

Braking his slide toward hysteria, Perry forced himself into silence, stalked off down the hallway. At least I didn't say god is in the details, Perry thought. Or the devil, or some other appalling cliché.

Perry's resistance to easy speech provided no comfort to him. He damned himself for ignoring his limits: he might be strategically gifted, a visionary, but he was tactically weak. He should have found another Milton, relied on him in this.

The Emperor broods upon the throne, thought Todd. Revolt flares in yet another province. Considering the document table's uncharted topography, Todd decided that the hunger for hegemony is ever the harshest master.

Twenty-five

Start a file on a body these days and data just dive right in. Thanks to freedom-of-information acts, the booming buyer's market in commercial mailing lists, and credit-reporting companies with security leakier than visitor control in public housing projects, the Langley Peach could tell Perry Stockbridge exactly what Brooks comma Todd Marquis and Feinberg comma Rollo No Middle Initial ate, drank, watched, read, slept in, slept on, and drove.

Hitchlessly, without any heavy lifting, the Peach assembled her simulacra of these two subjects. She complemented their familial, medical, professional, and financial histories, her paper records, with an audio-visual digitized archive, cross-referenced photographs, audiotapes, and videotapes.

As her records broadened and deepened, so did her pride in them, her protective affection for them. She labeled this a "displaced maternal instinct" and filed it, too, in her voluminous invisible dossier on herself.

All of these records, all of these observed and observable linkages, she delivered daily to Stockbridge. He did not ask for analysis, interpretation, intelligence *estimates*, so she kept her inferences from him.

The challenge, the true test of her method and mettle, was Blauser. When Stockbridge left him, Milton warped for a time outside the known universe, into the no-place of no-matter where the cursor blinks dumbly on "no data available." But she tracked him by his minimalist pleadings, his spoor, from his post-office box, to 1138 West Madison Street, to the Racine Street police station, and right on in to Athena's Arms, where she ordered a half carafe of diet cola and an appetizer plate of *saganaki*, *spanakopita*, and *dolmades*.

Whipped on by her compulsion to collect information, the Langley Peach closely questioned her waiter about ingredients and preparation. The waiter inferred — understandably, but wrongly — that the Peach was inflamed, *aroused*, by the food presented to her; he told Dimitrios the chef, who sized up her potential as a love-slave for himself, Dimitrios the *art*ist, who prepared it.

As Dimitrios sculpted Spiro's daily specials, carving slices of gyros from the rotisserie and filleting Lake Superior whitefish at the kitchen station in the middle of the dining room, he tried but failed to catch the Peach's eye with his, from under his single, forehead-spanning, blackly fierce Aegean eyebrow. He even left his culinary bunker to fire up her *saganaki* personally, with a six-inch jet of flame from his solid-gold lighter and an operatically basso "Opaa!" that won him applause and every heart in the room — but one.

Dimitrios retreated to his stage, stunned, humiliated, and utterly disgusted. The *hell* with American women! The bloody Delphic oracle was easier to understand! For some inscrutably female reason tied to her obvious frigidity (How could he have missed it?), the cretinous bitch at Table Six ignored him. She preferred to ogle the sixty-one-year-old busboy with the watery gray eyes and do-it-yourself lobotomy.

Instantly, Dimitrios decided to propose to his fifth cousin, imported recently from Delos to bear his children and inevitable philandering. Gallantly setting aside the issue of her mustache (which could be mooted anyway, with deft electrolysis), Dimitrios saw at last that his fifth cousin respected him, no, worshiped him. How could he have been so blind? And out of fairness to himself, even in this epiphany, he could not overlook his cousin's velvet thighs and plush chest, which this anorexic American clownette plainly lacked.

While Dimitrios rained silent curses on the women of his adopted culture, the Peach hoisted a final forkful of his excellent spinach cheese pie into her mouth and watched Milton work among the patrons. She remarked his noiseless removal of diners' debris and, more than that, his perfect timing. He was never early or late in setting places, filling water glasses, clearing dishes, supplying additional napkins, mopping up spills, bagging leftovers. Milton was, she realized, the consummate busboy: on his watch, nothing shattered, clattered, or spattered.

As the luncheon wave ebbed, Milton settled heavily on a chair at an undressed table next to the hallway leading to the restrooms. Why, thought the Peach, there's that horrid froggy man again. My, he just hops in *ev*erywhere!

Without looking at the waiter, the Langley Peach said,

"Baklava? Why, yes, I believe I will. But just the smallest piece, please. And coffee? Black? Thank you."

Sipping her coffee, moving her chair a few inches to achieve an unobstructed view of Milton's face past Pontiac McDowell's narrow sloping shoulder, the Peach pulled a stenographer's pad from her purse and began to write in shorthand on it, her eyes fixed on Milton's lips.

Twenty-six

Eyes closed, Milton welcomed the heat of the solstitial sun. It passed above the statue of Ceres on top of the Board of Trade building, warmed the bankers and traders and lawyers clotting the sidewalks along LaSalle Street. The weather cheered them, sung to them, called them out to hunt up lunch at high noon on a Thursday in the summer before the first Kennedy assassination.

"Mr. Blauser?" in a quiet baritone drew Milton out of his meditation in front of the entrance to the Federal Reserve Bank. Before Milton stood a tall, unsmiling, wheat-blond man-child, in navy blazer, yellow plaid sport-shirt open at the collar, black chinos, white socks, and black penny loafers. In his left hand, he held the right hand of a woman tall enough that the part in her hair was level with the young man's eyes. Wearing a white linen sundress, she, too, was blond, but not very, with brown eyes so dark they seemed all pupil even in the bright June sun. She looked athletic, a trim product of tennis and field hockey at one of the Seven Sisters.

"Perry Stockbridge," the young man said, holding out his hand. Milton unlocked his gaze from the woman, whom men loved deeply the instant after she first smiled at them. "I've looked forward to meeting you," said Stockbridge. "I'm graduating from Holmes next June. You spoke there on the Cuban missile crisis last fall. You were very persuasive."

"Thank you," Milton said, unable to recall which side he'd argued in the debate on blockades and blockheads.

"This is Lynette, my wife. We want to get married. You can help us."

"Well, uh," Milton said.

The woman laughed and said, "Oh, Perry. Give him a fair chance." She shook Milton's hand, too, with a firm dry grip, whispering, but playfully, so Perry could hear her: "He likes to be confounding."

Intent on proving her point, Perry continued: "You went to Harvard. You have your own practice, but you're pretty near broke, I hear." Perry smiled then. "So am I, but my wife is about as far from busted as you might get. So we can help you, too."

Planting his feet to keep his balance in the next shock-wave they might send his way, Milton asked, "You want to retain me?"

"In a sense, yes." said Lynette Stockbridge. "It's such a beautiful day. We'd love to walk and talk, rather than sit in that stuffy little Room 1461 in One North LaSalle Street. Together, we can demonstrate to Mr. O'Keefe that his doubts about the economies of his sub-lease to you are unfounded."

Milton's open mouth prompted Lynette Stockbridge to add this, lightly: "Thorough research provides a sound foundation for significant decisions." She reached for Milton's briefcase. "Let me carry this." She looked at her watch. "You don't have to be in court for another two hours. And it's an agreed motion anyway."

"Significant decisions," echoed Milton, catching on. "Your decisions."

"Yes," said Perry.

"Mine, too?" asked Milton.

"Oh, we think so," said Lynette Stockbridge, swinging Milton's briefcase. She linked arms with Milton, Perry at her other side. Through his jacket, his shirt, Milton felt the strength in her arm. In her.

"Our significant decisions," Milton said.

The three walked north along LaSalle to Monroe, then turned east. As they crossed Lake Shore Drive to the yacht club, a flock of gulls took flight and swooped around them.

They turned south at the water's edge, walked along the lakefront toward the aquarium. The midday sun shone down on sailboats and cabin cruisers, skiffs and dinghies, captains and crews scrubbing decks, polishing fittings, furling sails, spilling gas and martinis into the yacht basin.

"Professor Westin said you were a very good lawyer ... " Perry began in his soft voice.

"... but a very bad salesman," finished Lynette briskly, "for yourself. Your practice."

"We believe we can solve your business problem to our mutual advantage," Perry continued.

Lynette nodded. "I have a small amount of work. A claim against a company must be settled or tried." She smiled. "And there is more work. I am the chairman of these boards, you see. A number of infant corporations, toys, really, that I created. And a trust or two. I may want to make something of them."

"They're immature," added Perry, "but with potential for growth. But we can't be married ... " Perry began.

"... unless and until Perry can support me," finished Lynette. My father insists on that."

"But you are married," Milton pointed out. "You said so."

"Yes. We are," replied Lynette, smiling at Perry with such evident love that both of them glowed, "but not publicly. It's ... a secret."

"So," said Milton, parsing slowly, "he comes to work with me ... "

"... and I provide clientele and fees." Mocking amazement, Lynette made her eyes round. "*Large* fees."

"Only initially," Perry interjected severely. "And there will be real work, more than enough for you and me. This isn't a sham. It's a well-founded joint venture. A partnership."

Lynette smiled. "Perry will do what you tell him to do, learn what he can, and handle client ... relations." Lynette slipped her arm around Perry's waist.

"For how long?"

Airily, Lynette proposed, "'til death us do part'."

"Too long," said Milton, shaking his head, "or too short. Too uncertain."

"After our wedding," Perry said, "we can make agreeable terms."

"Fair." Milton nodded, frowned. "But how can you get married if you already are? There are records."

"Acapulco is even warmer than this in the winter," answered Lynette.

A second, distant male voice — "Hey, Milton, who is your friend here?" — interrupted these negotiations. "Spiro," said Milton, opening his eyes, surfacing from the past in a blink of them, "this is Mr. McDowell. A writer." Pontiac reached up and shook Spiro's hand. "He can help me with my building."

But that would be too easy, McDowell added silently, smiling benevolently, planning malevolently. This story is different from the one McDowell knew, the one McDowell told Brooks. Go back

40 years and look at things and they change. They *always* fucking change. They *mu*tate. Stockbridge pushed overboard this demented little *naif* with total recall — McDowell hoped — after Milton made it possible for the woman who loved Perry, the woman Perry loved, to marry him. The wealthy, beautiful, clot-throwing Lynette. Dead these 15 years, fatally stricken after the death of her only boy, oh boy, oh boy.

"You got another friend, too. A lady over there, she asked me to give you this." Spiro pulled a ten-dollar bill from his shirt pocket and held it out to Milton. "Maybe she's an angel, eh? She told me to say to you, you are a wonderful busboy. I told her I know that."

At that, McDowell whipped around in his chair. He saw only a busboy, resetting the unoccupied table to which Spiro pointed. Instead of handshakes all around, and a civil, traditional "Good bye," or "Nice meeting you," Pontiac McDowell stood up so quickly he knocked his chair over backwards, shouted, "Fucking Feinberg!" and ran out of the restaurant.

After this windfall, Milton needed only $9,393.00 to finance fully his redemption. A bargain, he reckoned, at twice the price. Yes.

Twenty-seven

In the situation room at D&W, a soundproofed, need-to-know, room-within-a-room with a sign on the inside of each door saying "Please close this door during meetings." Todd suddenly sneezed.

Suffering acute cephalic compression from a summer cold, bathed in fluorescence and air conditioning better suited to storing corpses, Todd wiped his nose raw, shivered, drew near to mourning his terminally bored mortal soul as intensely as he hated his profession. While the title drones buzzed around the room, emitting white noise on the issue of who — or just exactly what — owned Blauser's building at any given point in time, Todd shuffled woozily along the length of the situation-room table, to inspect still another Thorn and Texas media-clippings file.

Heartland Title and Trust had not yet settled ownership of Milton's hearth and hovel. Oh, it would, it would. Simon Smythe repeatedly popped up at Todd's side, assuring Todd that laying title to rest was only a matter of time and patience, "and a spot of money, hah, hah, hah."

Sir Simon the Wind-Sock operated on the pitiable misapprehension that he should regularly "liaise" with Todd — where the *hell* did Smythe think he was? — about the recession of Smythe's ignorance on the matter of title. Supposedly for Todd's benefit, Smythe advised — no, *way* too strong a word, "suspected" sat better and "guessed" was best — that 1138 West Madison crouched within the dark-star mass of Thorn and Texas assets, but no, wait, on the uh, the edge of it, well, maybe next to it, "ah, to be sure, Milton's tenement and Thorn and Texas certainly were ummm uh, *connected*", or had been once upon a time or twice or twenty, or, might be, no, *would* be, joined again, he should think, "Oh, yes, oh, most possibly."

"Certainly," burbled Smythe, "Our busy little B. conveyed 1138 West Madison outright to Thorn and Texas. More than once, yes more than once. And to subsidiaries, affiliates, and other entities with no apparent relationship to Thorn and Texas." Incredibly, "the mad mogul of Madison" — Smythe's alliterative whimsy, *not* Todd's — repeatedly found ready, willing, and able buyers over the years for slices of his building, trading away, for example, "a fee simple in the southwesternmost 40 cubic feet of the second floor of the subject property." Milton recovered these interests, although not always from the entities to which he had sold them, and he sold them again and again and again.

The title company had not conclusively scored Blauser's goofball game of hot potato, but the lodestar of Smythe's jack-in-the-box disquisitions was that any residual ambiguity was "ummm, uh, academic, I should think,": the acid bath of a tax deed proceeding would resolve all, clear the field, put the building in the hands of the land trust managed by FSGA. "Put paid, in short, to this little roundelay of our Mr. Blauser."

"Fine, good," snarled Todd, "now shut *up*!" Appalled by this breach of collegiality, Smythe turned on his heel and stiffened his upper lip, to cheer his stout lads *forward!* to the finish line.

Socked in from the neck north, Todd lacked time and heart for Heartland's piss-pot pusillanimity on the trivial matter of title. Perry had charged Todd to divine purpose and effect, order and rhythm, in Blauser's apparently random walk.

To annihilate that chaos, to find the fractals among the deals of Blauser and Thorn and Texas, Todd dug ever more deeply into transactions for Blauser's building. He needed the transaction documents themselves but he could not, would not, lay hands on them, unless Blauser or Thorn and Texas voluntarily disgorged them. That would not happen; neither Milton nor the target could be approached without unhorsing the ugly surprises planned for them, assuming they didn't already know.

Without the deal documents, Todd was forced to sniff down the title trail and through public bleatings about Thorn and Texas in business and trade journals. From the title search, Todd took the names of buyers and sellers of Milton's property that had a discernible relationship to Thorn and Texas. And from unidentified sources bruited in the press, Todd got Thorn and Texas deals. And were there *deals*! Past deals, current deals, future deals, on-again-off-again deals, diced, sliced, chopped, channeled, lost, tossed, and stir-fried deals.

Todd commanded the firm's librarian to perform database searches on all these entities. But, *but*, that downloading got him barely out of the blocks. Limning the cash, the goods, the intangible rights and duties, the *consideration*, flowing between

Blauser and Thorn and Texas for his entire building, or for the volume of space occupied by the rear door jamb, or for an easement across the fucking *roof!*, for Christ's sweet sake, led Todd by his dripping nose in countless bewildering directions.

As Todd found and read more and more about Thorn and Texas, the less he knew about it. There was, Todd found, no single Thorn and Texas paper trail to follow. There were paper *trails*, dammit, and they made Todd sicker and dizzier by the second.

Thorn and Texas didn't lead a linear corporate life. Hell, it wasn't even a two-dimensional mosaic. A transactional maelstrom, Thorn and Texas expanded in every direction, reached backward and forward in time, branching off, doubling back, taking both forks in the road, and then heading itself off at the pass. Todd couldn't decide whether Blauser's building or Thorn and Texas was riding off into the sunset or riding back *out* of the sunset, or was it the sunrise, because which the hell way was west?

Todd tacked little descriptions of Thorn and Texas transactions to the cork-lined wall that ran the length and height of the conference room, dates and times and arrows for transactions, running from left to right, but the wall wound up looking like an outsized ant colony — layers of overlapping descriptions with connectors running up, down, left, right, in and out from layer to layer. Todd continually repositioned the descriptors even as he rewrote them, like the little plastic tile-puzzles on keychains where the tiles are parts of pictures and they are mixed up and must be slid around to put them in order. Except the tiles in Todd's puzzle kept shifting and changing whenever they wanted to, materializing and vanishing. And all of the media coverage was without comment from anyone at Thorn and Texas, without even the bare public identification of any *officer* of Thorn and Texas.

Two associates from the corporate transactions group heard about Todd's work-wall, looked in, and left, sniggering. They saw he'd never figure out what the hell was happening at Thorn and Texas, and they had, therefore, one less rival in their associate class for making partner.

If Todd could just *concentrate*, he could grasp this greased pig, tackle it, take it *down*. But, he could *not* focus, because he could not *abide*, could not *handle*, any more distractions, such as voice mail messages from Pontiac McDowell and that butt-wipe Feinberg. Pontiac he could ignore, but then again, maybe he couldn't. Todd didn't know. Todd didn't know *anything*, really, except that listening to Mark read a great short story and achieving pretzel-magic intimacy with Louise didn't calm him or raise his resistance to the prevailing summer cold virus.

And he'd have to deal with the cop. Feinberg. The same cop who tied a can to Perry, jerked Perry's chain, ripped it right out of the toilet altogether. That little morsel o' current events was still ricocheting through D&W, murmured maliciously, nurtured mischievously, in the associates' lunchroom and the partners' dining room, growing from inquiry to arrest, from conviction to disbarment, from misdemeanor to Class X felony. The wheels of justice grind exceeding Feinberg.

Breaking and entering is a felony, Todd remembered. Feverishly, he tried to visualize locking his apartment before he left for work that morning, before he rode the el downtown at 6 a. m. with commodity traders snoring in $300 shoes and $5 ties and coffee-shop waitresses whose ankles retained far more water than they served to their regular customers. It did not comfort Todd that a thief who stole from him stole trash. Some trash was just too damn valuable to lose. Some trash was irreplaceable, okay? And a fucking claim on his homeowner policy for the value of his trash would boost his premium into the troposphere.

And why, Todd worried, was he suddenly so frightened about theft? *Property* is theft. What the hell was going on? And where the hell was it happening?

Wobbling to a fresh stack of clippings delivered from the library's on-line services, Todd focussed on the clipping on top, and he said, no, he *shouted*, "Oh, fuck, wait a minute! What the hell is *this*?" In his trembling right hand, in the silent space he instantly made for himself in that room, in that building, of his entire world, Todd lifted a clipping and read it. And read it again.

Todd tottered over to the wary Smythe and whispered, "1995 transactions. I'd like to see them again, please."

The clipping Todd clutched was a column by a business reporter dead two years of drinking and driving his Harley hog off the Monroe Street bascule bridge into the Chicago River. The newsieno-more's column stated that "Thorn and Texas, a privately held company, reportedly has purchased a stake in realty located at 1138 West Madison, in exchange for an ownership interest in T&T. The terms of the transaction were not disclosed."

In 1995, Milton had owned a piece of Thorn and Texas. All but certainly acquired for an easement in the second floor window sash, ho, ho, ho, or downstream riparian rights in rainwater flowing out the down spout on the north side of the building.

"Wait, wait, wait," muttered Todd, skull cracked open to admit a shaft of invisible light. "*Had* owned? Why *had* owned?" Did Milton have any *current* interest in Thorn and Texas?

Todd dug further that day, that night, the next day and night. He slept fitfully on a couch in the document room, lost his place in time and space. But, *but*, he grew ever more certain that Milton still had, *surely* still had, a piece of Thorn and Texas. Oh, yes.

Mad Milton, the manic magnate of Madison Street, *was* Thorn and Texas.

Twenty-eight

At 130 East Randolph Drive, a concrete promontory sloping up and east toward the Lake, overlooking Grant Park and the Illinois Central Railroad tracks aimed toward the South Side and south suburbs, the Chicago office of the Attorney Registration and Disciplinary Commission occupies the 31st floor of the original Prudential Insurance skyscraper, a smooth-faced, L-shaped box that had been the tallest in Chicago in the 1950s but now is only visible from the south along the lakefront.

Poignantly remorseful or stiffly unrepentant, shaking and drooling from high-powered tranquilizers or becalmed on a dead sea of despondency, the doomed, damned, and dim among the lawyers of northern Illinois journey to that building every business day. They bide a while in purgatory there, learn the return-date, if any, stamped on their licenses, launched by the A.R.D.C. into limbo for a month, a year, forever.

On Milton's express elevator ride up to the A.R.D.C.'s suite, his ears popped painfully and he swallowed hard twice to equalize the pressure on both sides of his eardrums. Rodding out his left ear with a cotton swab he stashed in his yellow satchel as the doors slid open, he stepped out of the elevator. All around Milton, a string trio sang Schubert on a concealed sound system, a notch above the subliminal level.

Even without a watch, he was on the dot for his 9:30 a.m. appointment with Joan Sczuliewski, a 63-year-old blue-rinsed widow in a gray cotton pant-suit. Sczuliewski was the A.R.D.C.'s first unmoved mover, the chief staff attorney, architect of 39 license-liftings over a 22-year career, including three alderman, six circuit court judges, and one sitting Attorney General.

However different her respondents' social stature, public profile, style or substance, whether they begged or offered bribes for mercy, whether they were mis-, mal-, or non-feasors, they all shared a fatal flaw: they were too damn dumb to cover their tracks. She alone could see them mounted on her walls, the invisible pelts and horns and heads of her kills: lawyers made out-lawyers for estate-raping, tax-evading, bribe-taking, evidence-suppressing, justice-obstructing, perjury-suborning, hit-ordering, or just lamely contributing to the reptilian reputation of the legal profession by blowing one or ten or twenty statutes of limitations on perfectly sound claims or defenses.

From the tip of the iceberg she surely sensed below the water line, Joan Sczuliewski happily scraped these scum. From the end of the behavioral bell-curve where the sinners lie (and where they also cheat and steal), she fire-hosed the trash she found in law, the trash found in every trade, craft, industry, art, and calling. At the other end of the bell-curve, her four sons and three daughters practiced law or judged those who did, diligently, scrupulously, and marrow-deep terrified of ever *seeing* their Mom, in a professional sense.

She loved her work, never wanted for work, and had *stories*. About respondents in interviews, depositions, and hearings who yelled, cursed, whined or cried; took Five, groveled, bluffed, or lied (and lied a second coat of lies in case they missed a spot). The woman who threatened to kill herself right in the middle of a hearing, held a gun to her head until Joan gently talked it out of her hand, and a guy who actually did, heaved the court reporter's stenography stand through the window, with the dervish motion of an Olympic hammer thrower, and dove out after it, which was when and why the A.R.D.C. switched to windowless hearing rooms.

Oh, the *truly* clever, quick and strong eluded her, but "Ain't it ever thus?" she asked. "At least I'm improving the breed."

Sczuliewski met Milton at reception and escorted him to her office. She offered him his choice of the chair by her door or the one next to her desk. With her desk's length parallel to the wall rather than perpendicular to it, Sczuliewski could share open space with her prey. A respondent in open space is at ease, hopeful, careless. Hung above her desk was a bulletin board covered with 48 candid pictures, in as many sullen poses, of her acutely spoiled four-year-old great-grandson. Behind her on the credenza beneath her window were a riot of healthy blooming plants, boosting the oxygen content in her office to an intoxicating level.

Sczuliewksi settled in her chair and swiveled it to face Milton, who chose the chair next to her desk. In a high, thin, by-cracky voice, she said, "It's helpful to come in so quickly." She pushed a plate of cookies toward him and pulled his file from a red-well jacket on her desk. Looking up from her letter to him, she said, "We invite respondents to visit informally because we realize this can be a very stressful experience. Orientation is helpful to them. This is a first complaint, I see. So, what questions do you have?"

"What happens to your name?" asked Milton. "Suhlooski, Shooloosky, Zoolooski, Skuhzooleeooski?"

"All of the above," the investigator replied, content to let Milton small-talk his way toward the allegations against him.

"More Polish persons here than anyplace but Warsaw," Milton said. "What's so hard about Sczuliewski?" Milton took a moment to admire her office. "Open floor plan," he observed. "Warm. Inviting." He looked closely at one of the plants behind her. "'Dumb cane.' The sap of *diefenbachia amenum* is poisonous. Keep an eye on the boy when he's here." Pointing to the salutation of her letter to him, Milton said, "It's not Baluser," Milton said, "it's Blauser. B then l then a. Not B then a then l."

Sczuliewski looked over her glasses at her letter to Milton and compared it to the copy of Stockbridge's letter to the A.R.D.C.. "Oh, dear, so it is. I'm sorry."

"And I know what you do. How you do it. *Why* you do it." Joan Sczuliewski was uncomfortably unsure whether Milton meant the A.R.D.C. or her, personally. "I don't have any questions about that," Milton said, shaking his head. "No."

After a pause that grew awkward only for Sczuliewski, she looked down at her notes in the file, cleared her throat. "Well. The complaint alleges you knowingly commenced baseless litigation."

"Wrong," said Milton, "wrong, wrong, wrong."

Ah, denial, thought Sczuliewski, *terra cognita*. Comfortable again, she asked for an explanation.

Milton put his right forearm on the corner of her desk. He said, "Okay. Theory of the case: ... " And Milton talked. He linked up every alleged fact to each cause of action in the complaint. His pellucid discourse became an epic poem, an oratorio. He explained how each of his arguments and cases refuted the shallow and hilariously specious submissions of his adversary.

Sczuliewski laughed with Milton until she whooped and wheezed. When he ended, when she caught her breath, she quickly agreed, "Absolutely! But why didn't the judge get this? It's very straightforward."

"She is a very nice person."

"But not real smart?"

"Oh, no. No. Very smart." Milton sighed, looked down at his hands in his lap. "Unfocussed. Divided. Wanted to win, wanted to lose. *Tried* to lose."

When she realized he was talking about himself and not the judge, which took time without her hearing any pronouns, Sczuliewski quietly said, "That's unprofessional."

Milton shook his head. "Client knew. Didn't mind."

"Tolerant client," she wondered, slipping into Blauser's syntax. "Do you have any documentation for this disclosure to the client?"

"Don't need any."

She made a note on the file jacket. "Because ... ?"

"The client's a fool."

The dusk outside her window surprised her. "You're the client," she said.

"Yes." He grimaced apologetically. "Forfeited a winning position. Always *win* them. I'm appealing."

"You are, dear," said Great-grandmother Sczuliewski, nudging the china plate toward him. "Another cookie?"

Twenty-nine

At 10:38 p.m, Todd shoveled his Thorn and Texas notes into his desk drawer, slammed it shut and locked it. Todd needed a drink and Louise, who'd called and asked to meet him in the lobby.

Todd rode down alone in the elevator, bouncing lightly on his heels to the bonging of the floor indicator, surfing on a surfeit of caffeine and sugar standing in for food, rest, clean underwear and any sign, from any quarter, of genuine humane interest in his personal growth and development.

In the vaulted lobby, he saw Louise, but Mark was with her. "Hey," Todd said. "Where's the party? Or are you the party?" Todd caught his right heel at the rise of a gray terra cotta floor tile, tripped, staggered, mumbled "Whoops," righted himself. "Let's go, okay? Wherever. I'm stupider than usual."

Mark pushed first through the revolving door, then Louise, then Todd, who went around an extra time to goose his centrifugal momentum. On the street, knifing through the acrid fug produced by the firm's overnight secretaries on their cigarette break, Louise said, "There's a cab."

They settled into the back seat, Louise on the hump, Mark on her right, Todd on her left. Thigh to thigh to thigh to thigh. Mark leaned away from Louise, watched out the rear window over his left shoulder.

"Are you important?" Louise asked Todd.

Bewildered, he twisted to look at her, rammed his behind painfully into the door handle, and answered, "To what? Who? Excuse me, whom?"

"At work. What you're doing."

"Oh," Todd said, "I'm in*comp*arably important. In the slime-at-the bottom-of-the-food-chain sense. Got all the answers to the cosmic questions. That's all you need to know, Ms. Need-to-know. But," he held up a finger to his lips, "I've babbled enough. I can say no more, with Mr. O'Henry here and all. Mr. Short Story. He's not on this case. *Our* case." Todd leaned forward and looked across Louise to Mark. "Have to invoke the attorney-client privilege, man. Lower the cone of silence. Sorry about that, chief."

"Jesus," muttered Mark.

"I met this woman at the club," said Louise, "on the squash challenge court. Couple days ago. We talked."

"'Girls talk,'" sang Todd. "'If you want to know hooooowwww, girls talk.'" He peered over at Louise. "Was she a Lindsay? Just curious." He leaned forward to look past Louise at Mark. "Everybody in her fucking club," — the cabdriver, a turbaned Sikh named Reginald Pal-Singh, winced and scowled up at Todd in his rear-view mirror — "is a Lindsay. Or a Whitney. Or," he ticked off each on his fingers, "Courtney, Tyler. First-name last-names. Gordon. Hunter. *Not* Tiffany or Kimberly. No. Too down-market. And no Kelly, please. Spare me. Too, you know, *ethnic*."

"Jane," said Louise.

"Really? *Jane?*" asked Todd.

"Let's just call her Jane, okay? Names don't matter!"

"Please, no shouting in the cab," said the driver, pulling over to the curb just east of Dearborn. He half-turned in his seat to glare at Louise.

"Sorry," said Louise.

"And no more cursing," said Pal-Singh, "or I throw you out. This is where I work, you know? Twelve hours a day. And pray. Would you like it if I started yelling and blaspheming where you work? In your temple?"

"Yes," said Todd, "but I understand that's not your point. We'll be good. Okay?"

Marginally mollified, Pal-Singh started up again.

"I can't tell," said Mark to Louise.

"Can't tell *what*?" asked Todd.

"Are you important?" Louise asked Todd again.

"Fuck if I know," Todd countered.

No idle threatener, Pal-Singh pulled over to the curb again, at Wabash and Monroe. "Out! Now!" He picked up a cellular phone, brandished it at them. "Or I call the police. Out!"

The three lawyers climbed out of the cab as an elevated train clattered above them. Mark looked at his watch and then at Louise. "I'm going home." Looking at Todd, Mark thought, by myself and fuck you too. Mark started off toward Michigan Avenue, to find still another cab, a quiet cab for one, please, far from the bandstand and the kitchen.

Louise pulled Todd into a doorway by his lapels. Clumsily, Todd tried to put his arms around her but she blocked him with her forearms, pushed him roughly against the opposite wall and backed away. "The hell's going on here?" asked Todd. "What do you want? What do you want me to want?"

She didn't answer immediately, so Todd said, "Oh, fuck this," and took a step out of the doorway. Louise lunged out after him, wrapped her arms around his chest from behind, pulled him back into the doorway. He tried to turn in her arms, but she broke away, backed toward the wall opposite her. "We were talking about men," she said, breathing hard.

"'We'? Who?"

"Jane and I."

Light-headed, Todd stuck his hands in his jacket pockets, slumped back against the wall. "Men?"

"And we started talking about ... *beaus*."

"Bows?" asked Todd. Bewildered, he began listing to his left, wracked by fatigue so deep that the backs of his thighs and calves ached, whacked giddy by occasional whiffs of Louise as the wind swirled in the doorway.

"You know." Louise looked away. "How men are impossible, but possible."

Smiling, Todd started toward her again, raising his arms to embrace her, feeling a rare cheap rush of potency: a tough, beautiful woman was about to say she loved him, loved Todd Marquis Brooks, even with all his flaws, all his San Andreas-sized faults. Yes, yes, *yes!*

"Don't," Louise warned, pointing her right index finger in the general direction of his adam's apple. "Get back over there. And, god, be quiet." Reluctantly, regretfully, Todd retreated, allowed his arms to drop to his sides.

"We compared notes," Louise continued. Boyfriend this and boyfriend that ... "

Todd waited her to smile or blush or avert her eyes modestly when she faded out, but she didn't, and Todd thought, oh, shit. This callous calculating bitch disemboweled him for the amusement of strangers. His heart chilled, hardening to her.

"... after a while," Louise continued, "we were talking about you. Only about you." She was so interested in you, I began to feel ... possessive. Territorial."

Todd decided Louise was bent on herding him to hell by cattle prod to his heart. Or was she dangling him over the Pit by bungee cord wrapped around his scrotum? Oh, no matter. The road to his damnation surely was their moaning sweating rocking shouting, their tangled exhausted release, their bodies covering each other and then falling away.

Louise stopped, ran her eyes down from his matted mouse-brown hair, past his glassy eyes, oily-shiny nose, slack jaw, stained shirt and tie, wrinkled suit, and scuffed shoes. "Are you sleeping?"

Feeling a tic starting in the right corner of his right eye, Todd rubbed it with his right index finger. "Sure. I curl up at the office. Under my desk, on a table. You know how it is." He smiled wanly. "Feed the monster, pay the bills."

Louise said, "She didn't want to know why I liked you. Oh, she did, but not to be friends with me. Not to get to know me. I think what she really wanted was to know you. *Know* you."

"'She'? Oh, right. Back to your Jane person. Plain Jane. The Grand Inquisitor. Ms. Tor-que-ma-da — ." Todd said slowly, syllable then beat then syllable, so as not to stumble on it " — is spying on me? Fine. My life's an open book. She's welcome to it. Every blank page in it, thank you very much."

"If I were you, I'd be concerned."

Todd yawned, shrugged. "I stink and I'm hungry, but I'm on work-release. Your point here's what? And, speaking of here, can we leave now? This doorway doesn't have a liquor license. No kitchen, no menu. No tables, no cutlery, no chef's specials, no dessert tray, no sound system, no waiters, excuse me, *servers*. Where does this leave us? Am I making myself clear, here, in this doorway? Am I actually talking? Are we, in fact, *in* this doorway at — " he squinted at his watch " — 11:14 p.m.?"

Bleakly, Louise said, "You *are* stupid, Todd. But not any more than usually."

Todd's sputtering synapses next related inward how Louise left him in that doorway: without another word to him, for him, about him. "At least she didn't say goodbye," he muttered. That was the good news. But she was rude, as rude as he. Todd shook his head, wondered whether she took on protective coloration around her lovers, assumed their habits to camouflage herself. Did she identify with all her oppressors? Suffer from Stockholm syndrome? Did she treat all her lovers that way, or just her lovers like Todd, who were stupid enough, rude enough, important enough, to be followed?

Todd peered around the edge of the doorway, out onto Wabash, feeling scared and foolish for feeling scared. He swung his head south to north, saw a bearded black man in a tattered red sweat shirt riding up and torn jeans riding down to reveal a dirty white tee-shirt stretched tightly, incompletely, over his gut. The man slowly pushed a shopping cart filled with plastic garbage bags south along Wabash, stopping at street-corner wastebaskets. He used a long stick to churn through the trash until he struck aluminum cans. With the hook at the end of his stick, he fished them out and bagged them. The black man's plastic bags were packed.

Sweet, thought Todd. No license, no limit, and the cans are biting.

And while we're at it, fuck this too, thought Todd. If someone wanted to bag *his* can, say, what the hell could he do about it?

Todd tucked in his shirt, buttoned his collar, tightened his tie, squared his shoulders, and sauntered out of the doorway. Five doorways to his right, a car started, and Todd did, too. The sound of the engine drew Todd's eyes to the car, but its headlights remained dark. The car idled on, with no visible driver. I am not in Sleepy Hollow, Todd told himself. Someone somewhere was using a remote starter. This was mere coincidence, without meaning for him. He forced himself to walk slowly away from the car without looking back at it, wishing his wing-tips were wings.

At home in his studio condominium, Todd locked all the locks behind him, turned on all the lights, fed his fish, stripped off his clothes as he walked to the bathroom, turned on the shower, climbed in, showered. He toweled himself off and ran a tub in which to soak himself, especially his rude and stupid head.

Waiting for the tub to fill, Todd punched the replay button on his answering machine. In front of the open refrigerator, spooning peanut butter from a jar directly into his mouth, he listened to Pontiac McDowell whisper, "Time to deal, fuckhead."

With whom? Todd wondered, licking the spoon. And for what?

Thirty

On its seventh anniversary, the interior of Stockbridge & Blauser, the physical plant of the firm, reflected Perry's business plan (though it had no such name): deploy Lynette's capital to secure the confidence of clients. In reception, each office, and the conference rooms, there were original modern art and curvilienar teak furniture, amber Persian rugs and coffee-velvet curtains. In the library, a graduate of Balliol presided over a complete and current collection of Illinois and federal statutes and reports. A fresh coat of cream paint was applied every six months to each wall in that time when everyone smoked everywhere, except Milton, who did not smoke at all. Window air conditioners hummed in every office, electric typewriters on every desk, except Perry's, because he did not type at all.

Each attorney — the two partners and their six associates, one added each year — had his Ivy League summer clerk, suspendered, bow-tie over starched white shirt under herringbone three-piece tweed, imperturbable young Brahmins tempered by service in college work-study programs as Congressional aides. These clerks kept in touch, usefully, with their legislative mentors, and their older brothers in their families' investment banking houses in Boston and New York.

At first, all the firm's business was charged to Lynette's account: vetting her nominees for joint ventures; fixing terms agreeable to her and her partners; drafting her contracts; suing and trying or settling her deals that did not progress as predicted or promised. This transactional work, detailed in crisp, careful prose, and the litigation that fell out of it, impressed Lynette's co-venturors, who delivered additional business to the firm if not sued by it.

Lynette's proposed division of labor persisted. Perry socialized with prospective clients, interviewed them, asked the questions Milton taught him, the lawyer's time-tested questions: what did the client want? what would it accept? when did it want results? when would it need them?

On behalf of the firm, Perry accepted only those assignments that passed a stringent three-part test: first, would the client pay a $10,000 non-refundable retainer, irrespective of any services to be rendered? second, would the client escrow an amount equal to the firm's estimated fee for services to be rendered, payable as and when demanded? third, how did the prospective client expect to prevail in the matter at hand?

"Prevail" was the slippery term in the last question, which was Perry's contribution: it encompassed winning, of course, but also losing and drawing, and slowly or quickly. A prospective client had to appreciate the precise position and purpose of its legal work in its business strategy. What was the client's interest in its competitors? Was the client anti-trust, or, well, pro-trust? How high did it want the barriers of entry to its markets, how could it justify their height, and how did it expect to raise or lower them? Clients were referred elsewhere if they ceased to answer these inquiries with the kind of clarity they expected of Stockbridge and Blauser on their behalf.

Perry transcribed their answers in a cryptic private language for Milton, who planned and supervised the firm's professional labor for the clients they accepted. Perry unconditionally relied on Milton to select tactics and fora for their clients, as fully as Lynette trusted Milton to manage her affairs.

"My doctor," Lynette told Milton, "my obstetrician, says it is not uncommon for expectant women to become ... distracted. Scattered. I can't concentrate on business anymore, and I don't care to." Prenatally languid, she sipped from a glass of iced coffee. "My perspective is ... liquid." She smiled. "Cash me out, Milton. Make me altogether liquid."

Milton swiveled in his chair, took a ledger from his credenza. He turned back to face her, leafed through the accounts book to the last page, the most recent entry. "The *res* is $14,008,512.44. I don't know today's earnings. There have been trades, I know that, but they haven't cleared."

"That's quite a bit improved from last quarter. You've been the beaver. I'm proud of you." Lynette's surprise, her pleasure, seemed genuine, but Milton could not tell, could never tell. On an impulse — uncommon for her, but less so as she advanced further in her pregnancy — Lynette added, "Please keep ten percent of the principal. As your bonus beyond your management fee. You've earned it, down to the penny."

Blauser thanked her, blushed for her. He did not question her decision or ask if she'd discussed it with Perry. Lynette had made it plain to Milton that Perry had no role in her business; she would not have married him if he wanted any part of what she had. Perry received nothing but the benefits she provided upon formation of the law firm, and he only took them to accomplish their public marriage. When the firm was profitably established, when Perry's independent income was secure, he paid back every penny and insisted that Lynette provide no more money to him. As investment banker and counselor, Milton entirely handled her account during the term of the partnership, and Perry never inquired about it.

Milton asked Lynette, "Do you have plans for the proceeds?"

"I might, someday," she teased. She traced a circle on her stomach. "A trust for this one, I think. Yes."

"Do you want me to act as trustee?"

"No, Milton, I do not. Oh, don't look hurt. I just want to be friends, now."

Not enough, thought Milton.

"And you have this practice," said Lynette. "You must look after it. You and Perry depend on each other. He's ceased to require my support." To an unforeseen extent, Lynette feared. Perry was always with clients, building the firm, taking care to prove each day that Lynette had given her love wisely.

Milton asked, "Why not keep all the money in the business?"

"It would tempt me to pay attention to it. That time is past. I'm putting the principal in municipal bonds, tax-free brainless triple-As, in that good gray bank up the street." She looked up past his head out into late afternoon light, the orange radiance warming the western faces of the upper floors of taller buildings across LaSalle Street. "Interest will be good enough for her. Or him. I wish I knew." She smiled. "I call it 'Little X.' Just like a militant."

"We'll have to wind up the business."

"I won't let you. I'm giving it to you. I insist you cultivate it for yourself as well as you ran it for me." She stood up. "That's my gift to you, Milton, and my charge to you. You must care for it, if you care for me. As you care for me."

Not nearly enough, thought Milton, lifting his head from his hands. He blinked, pointed to the previous day's final account entry for Thorn and Texas. Net worth: $70,964,076.00, give or take that afternoon's six-month treasury-bill swings.

"Sweet holy mother of God," breathed McDowell, reclining on a sofa made of yellowing briefs, awed and chilled, to the bony knees sticking out of his camouflage shorts, by the presence of much more money than even he controlled. "What's that? That's — "

"— One point four million compounding at 17 percent per year for 25 years," Milton finished. "Within one standard deviation of average market performance for the period."

"For Christ's sake, Milton," Feinberg urged, "loan yourself a few grand. Pay the frigging taxes. You'll pay it back."

Obdurate, Milton shook his head. "Fruit of the poisonous tree."

"What?" said McDowell.

"Oh, don't say that," pleaded Feinberg. "The Fourth Amendment's got nothing to do with this. She gave you the business."

"Fucking A, she gave you the business," McDowell snorted. "Fucking Triple A. Yeah, just give yourself the money." No! Pontiac screamed silently. Don't do it! Don't fuck up the story!

"It was her money," said Milton. "Her money started it. Started everything that went wrong. I don't want it. I don't want it in my building. It's the fruit of — "

"Shut up, Milton," snapped Feinberg. "Give him the money, Pontiac. He's good for it."

"I won't," McDowell said quietly, eyes gleaming.

"I can throw your ass in jail, McDowell. *Jail.* You're in the showers, your ugly ass's up for grabs — "

"Just give it up, okay? Nobody's going to want my ass, and you wouldn't do it, anyway. False arrest shit'd fuck with your self-esteem. Besides, I'll get him the money."

"You will," sighed Milton. "I knew you'd help. I told Spiro you would."

"Oh, I will." Instantly, McDowell had their entire attention. "It's a lock. I write about Milton. The public pities him. Outpouring of cash follows. Milton redeems building. Works every time."

"I see a fly here," Rollo said slowly. "He's not your little welfare granny living in a refrigerator box, gumming dog food.

He's a millionaire. Who the hell's going to give nine thousand bucks to a frigging millionaire?"

Pontiac shrugged carelessly. "I don't know. A billionaire, maybe. That's not my problem."

"Worse," argued Rollo, "a millionaire *lawyer*. Hell, he's even got a day job. You wouldn't give nine large to him when you thought he was broke!"

"Please ... " implored Milton.

Patiently, McDowell said, "I don't give money to lawyers. You know that. Or wannabe lawyers." McDowell shrugged. "Besides, he's not a millionaire. Milton, are you a millionaire?"

"No."

"There you go," McDowell beamed at Rollo. "Happy?"

Feinberg stood up, shouted, "You got 70 million dollars on the books, you little ... aah!" He stomped out of Milton's room, slammed the door. On his way down the stairs, Rollo yelled, "The hell with this! The hell with *you*!" On tiptoes, Milton leaned over a stack of files, watched Rollo drive away from the second-floor file drawer in which Milton lived. He turned to McDowell.

"Hungry?" McDowell mildly asked Milton.

Surprised, Milton said, "Yes. Yes, I am."

"Good. Let's get some food. "But," he warned Milton, "I'm not paying for you. And I'm not giving you nine grand. You understand that?"

Distracted, Milton nodded, muttered, "Principal matter's a matter of principle." Anxiously, he added, "Detective Feinberg is distressed."

"He'll get over it," McDowell said in his most unctuously soothing voice. "He'll come around. He just doesn't understand yet. The poor are very different from you and me. We have to do this right, or not at all." And, as they emerged from the building, McDowell asked Milton, "What's the deal with the yellow bag?"

Thirty-one

The probative evidence from anthropology, the good evidence, the *hard* evidence, proves that humans are diurnal: taverns in Chicago have 4 a.m. licenses so that fearsome dark can be fended off, placated, displaced by rite with *light*, however sodden the supplicants, however much the lighted places stink of cigarettes and beer, and piss and fear.

At Danville & Williamston, uncomplaining machines served as Perry's acolytes in his ritual for banishing the night. At 11:00 p.m., as it did every evening, the monitor on his desk split its image into six equal fractions the size and shape of wish-you-were-here postcards, one for each office in the Kennel. The pinhole video cameras embedded in the walls and ceilings showed him *three* occupied offices, but only *two* associates still at work, no, *apparently* at work, *presumptively* at work, given the benefit of the doubt only until more was known. One associate read cases; the other processed words. A third associate slept at his desk, head sideways on his foam-rubber mouse-pad, a trickle of drool coursing down along his cheek onto the rough synthetic cloth covering the pad's surface. A fourth associate, the most junior pup in the Kennel, D&W's latest hire, furtively slipped into view in the sleeping lawyer's office.

On Perry's couch, the Peach crossed her bare legs under her and ran a finger through the condensation on her frosted mug of freshly squeezed orange juice mixed with ginger ale. "A journalist?"

Still watching the screen, admiring his *very* promising protégé reading the sleeper's mail, Perry said, "Hardly. A gossip monger."

"This isn't Central America."

"He intends to publicize my practice. I am in *private* practice. This is a plain breach of my privacy."

Unimpressed, the Peach yawned. "Don't puff up like a pigeon, dear. We're way past the mating dance."

"But I've retained you to assure my privacy."

"There are no real secrets," the Peach demurred. "The marketplace is a fishbowl. It puts a premium on information. You know, anything that reduces uncertainty?"

Perry probed. "This is not negotiable, then?"

"No, it is not," the Peach answered firmly. "Honey, if you just want him *done*, you don't need me. I know a dozen Balkan cowboys'd do him for a dollar. A couple a hundred Russians, too. I, in contrast, do not take orders merely to fill them. I am not a waitress. You purchase my obedience to my good judgment. Not my submission to your whims?" She sipped her orange juice. "Besides, I'll bet you didn't even think on the impact of his decommissioning on his stakeholders."

"'Stakeholders'?" Perry snorted. "MBA codswallop. How would anyone know? And why would anyone care?"

"I might tell on you."

"You? Why on earth would you do that? That would be a breach of our contract."

"Once more, unto the breach, breach, breach," she mocked him, coyly smiled at him over the rim of her glass. "What if you spurn me, darling, break my heart, leave me weeping at the altar?"

"You have nothing to fear from me," said Perry, rising from his chair behind his desk. He walked over and kneeled next to her, leaned toward her. Embraced her.

In his arms, the Peach put her hands on his chest, and grabbed two hands full of his shirt. "Undress," she whispered, having none of *that* left to do herself. "Slowly! We're not going anywhere, are we?"

When he slid under her, into her, she looked down at him. "We'll stay here all night," the Peach murmured, running her nails up the sides of his rib cage, "like Milton. Just," she gasped, "like," she panted, then screamed, "Milton!" She leaned down over him, her eyelashes tickling his nose, her nipples grazing his, and whispered, "There are no secrets." Later, the Peach shrieked, "We! Are! *Everywhere*!!!" and collapsed against Perry, knocking the wind out of him.

Afterward, as she slept in his arms, Perry smiled down at her. Stroking her hair, he concluded, not for the first time, that women achieve perfection when they lose their baby fat from their bodies and their minds. The Peach could be tediously didactic, but she was sharp, candid, and creative. He shivered from remembered pleasure. *Amazingly* creative.

She was right, of course — again! — to save him from coarse and artless impulse. Kidnaping and murder were the tools of common thugs and terrorists, amok in third world alleys where raw sewage ran in the gutters.

Perry knew and appreciated the momentum of money. Best, then, to rely on its inertia. It would crack Milton like an egg, perhaps unspectacularly, but certainly. Legally. The way of the ghost.

On the screen, Perry's most junior subordinate copied names from the rolodex of their sleeping colleague. Striking the *coup de morte* as he left his senior colleague's office, the new boy switched off the sleeper's desk-lamp left on to signal — *falsely* signal — midnight oil burning brightly for the firm.

At the hiring committee meeting in the morning, Perry argued for gene-typing reports on all applicants for entry-level associate positions. There could be useful data there, and he couldn't have too much of it.

Thirty-two

Spiro kept an office at Athena's Arms, the World Headquarters of Athena Trading Enterprises, "LLC.," whatever that meant. It occupied the northeast quarter of the second floor of his building and offered a breathtaking view of the Loop, especially when late afternoon light painted the western face of every building the color of Georgia clay.

Instead of working (with or without quotation marks) in his office, or even sleeping in it, Spiro filled it with restaurant supplies. He stacked laundered tablecloths on his desk, surrounded it with cartons of toilet paper, hand towels, and five-gallon drums of hand soap.

Spiro preferred to meet investors, inspectors, purveyors, and lawyers — the only people who sought him out at Athena's were dowsing his cash flow — at Booth One of his restaurant. There, he could see his kitchen and cash register and Heidi, his comely dining room hostess, who swore to him in bed that she had no — what was it she called them? — oh yes, "designs on his material estate." She actually used that phrase. "Designs"! Her overheated vocabulary was part of the price he conceded for hiring college graduates with theater degrees to greet his clientele.

Despite her express disinterest in his cars and buildings and boats and cash, despite the oils and candles and fervent physical entertainments, the words "pre-nuptial agreement" bolted and welded themselves to Spiro's vision of his future with Heidi, if they had one. Like all successful entrepreneurs, Spiro learned from his mistakes, but his hard-won, bone-deep caution in the terms and conditions of marriage clashed starkly with his abject failure to ask any questions about her deployment of birth-control devices, or use any himself, which demonstrated the broad ambivalence he expressed after hours to Milton, in Booth One.

Spiro sighed and said, "There are days, Milton. There are days when I want to make all of this" – he waved a hand at his domain — "disappear. Go back to my village. You know?"

Milton sat with Spiro as Spiro sat with his father, many years earlier, at the single sidewalk table of his father's business, their village's only café, with a glass of ouzo as the world unfolded to him, amid men's laughter and curses and complaints about business and politics and women.

Milton stared into and through the glass of ouzo on the table in front of him, roused himself from the bending of light within it to say, "Can be done. Has been done."

"She is so young," Spiro breathed. "So young. And so beautiful. And she asks for nothing. Nothing!" Spiro scowled. "That will change. She will want everything. She will *take* everything. Everything! Everything that *bitch* does not get!" He backed out of his post-nuptial rage long enough to say, "'Can be done.'? What're you saying? What can be done?"

Delphically, Milton murmured, "This. That."

Spiro shook his head, said, "Oh, no, my friend. No. No word games. I'm not ... educated. I don't understand what you're saying."

Milton said, "Gone but here. Here but there. Beyond there. Inaccessibly here and there." He looked up and into Spiro's eyes, added, "The easy part of it. With ... trusts," remembering more each day, Milton thought, like FSGA, Quality is Vision, I change the shape of things, "for charitable — "

"Wait, wait, wait." Spiro held up a hand to stop the accelerating avalanche of language. "You're telling me I have to give away my property ... " Spiro foundered on the alien enormity of the appalling idea, " ... *give away* my property? To charity?" Spiro shook his head, to clear it, "No, no, no. No. I built all this. I *created* it. I will not give it away. Even to stop that bitch from stealing it. That is against ... against ... *every*thing."

Milton nodded. "Okay. Don't give it away. Don't have to. Just impose ... discipline. The demands on the res. Structure." Noting Spiro's expression, Milton added, "'Res' is the things. Your things. Your property.."

Spiro leaned in toward Milton, asked softly, "Is this what you have done? For yourself?"

"Not for me," Milton answered quickly. "No. *Not* for me."

"You know what I mean." Spiro turned to the bar, shouted, "Alex!" and held up two fingers. The bartender looked up, nodded and brought them two more tumblers half-full or half-empty with ouzo and two more filled with water. Spiro poured water into his

ouzo and watch the mixture cloud itself. He raised his glass to
Milton, said "Yassoo," and drained half of it. He motioned to
Milton to follow him. Milton reversed the process, pouring ouzo
into water, because he could, and watched the ouzo sink and
spread and curl like smoke. He raised his glass to Spiro and sipped
it.

Milton said, "Different purpose. Different process."

"I am not challenging you, Milton. I accept what you say. But
what you do is ... hard. To do. To understand. You know? It is not
what I do. Not what I do."

Spiro added more water to his ouzo and drank half of the half
that remained in his glass. He stood, swayed as the ouzo charged
out of his stomach and into his blood stream, placed his hand on
the table to steady himself. "Drink up, my friend. Come with me.
We will go, we will go ... to my boat."

"What about ... where is ... ?" Milton fumbled for the name of
the young woman on whom Spiro determined to throw himself.

"Heidi?" Spiro snorted. "She is at a play. Or audition. Or
rehearsal. I gave her the night off."

"Seeking her muse."

"Eh? Her ... oh. Yes."

The shape of content, thought Milton, permits the sight of it.

Outside Athena's Arms, Spiro hunted in his jacket for his keys,
but didn't find them. "So! We will take a cab. I will pay. We will
spend the night on my boat." He took hold of Milton's sleeve as
the little man edged away. "Do not argue with me, Milton."

Spiro locked his arm through Milton's, waved at cabs on
Halsted heading south until one stopped for them. They rode a
mile farther to Roosevelt Road, past the Chicago campus of the
University of Illinois, a collection of angular symmetrical
buildings by architects trained in the post-60s, sniper-window
school of urban academic design. Their cab continued east one
mile to Lake Shore Drive, turned south on to the Drive and then
east again, passing between the Field Museum and Soldier Field to
the marina on the south side of the Adler Planetarium, filled with
large white yachts bristling with radar and two-masted sailboats
with their sails rolled away.

The air and water were calm. Spiro and Milton hardly staggered as they boarded *Zeus's Daughter*, neither the largest nor the smallest cabin-cruiser in the marina. It was well-tended and clean, with dark wood trim. They settled at a banquette and table built into the wall of the stern, beneath a wine-red canopy. From a cabinet beneath the cushions of the banquette, Spiro produced another bottle of ouzo and two glasses and poured them drinks. "We will drink to ... what?"

Milton looked around and up and pointed, "Moon."

"Yes," said Spiro. "The moon"

They raised their glasses and emptied them and filled them again and emptied them again. "To the water," said Milton.

Spiro nodded. "The Lake."

"Yes," said Milton. "*This* Lake. The beautiful Lake."

Spiro started to fill their glasses again, but Milton stayed his hand. Spiro said, "We have had enough?"

Milton nodded.

"Good," said Spiro. "We know." He looked up at the inverted L of the eastern face of the Loop bounding Grant Park, the long line of the L extending north and south, the short line east-west, lit at random, except for the band of white around the highest floors of the Hancock building. He waved his hand, tilted his head back, and squinted, so the lights diffracted through his lashes. "Beautiful."

"Yes," said Milton.

Spiro said, "No one owns what we see. No one owns it. It is free to us. And the people on the other boats. And out there? More free!" Spiro slipped off his loafers and socks and watched himself wiggle his toes. "This is good, Milton. I'm glad we're here tonight. Together." He looked at Milton closely. "I trust you. You work for me, but you don't lick my boots. Thank you." Spiro took off his jacket.

Milton said, "Don't."

Spiro said, "I ... " and stopped. Dropped his chin to his chest. Closed his eyes. He ran his right hand over his bald spot, touched it with the tips of his fingers, said, "I am tired. I see what I have and I don't ... I don't want it. I thought I knew, Milton. Not from school. From work, you know? From life. Not from school. I had to leave it to work. When I was ten. *Ten*, Milton! But it ... I'm ... stupid. Foolish. Old. You know? *Stupid*! I pretend to myself, *myself!* —

Spiro hit himself in the chest with a clenched fist — I have learned from life, from my life. From this, what to do. I pretend to be young. With Heidi." He looked out at the water, light lying and bent on it. "I am lost in this."

Milton said, "Please." He placed his hands on the table, palms up, and looked down at them, looked up at Spiro. He wiggled his fingers. Shrugged. "I ... Nothing in them. Empty." He closed them into fists, opened them again. "Still empty. We work with these. With their ... perfection. Wait." Milton tilted to the side, balancing on one haunch, extracted his wallet from his pocket. "Here," he said. "Look." Out of it he pulled a sliver of paper, a fortune from a cookie, sharply creased and faded. He slid it across the table to Spiro. "Read."

Spiro picked it up, held it up to catch the moonlight. Squinted to try to read it. "'To ... have' ... "

Milton prompted him: "' ... a friend.'"

"Ah. 'To have a friend, you must, you must ... '" Spiro held it away from his face. "I can't read it. It is too faded."

"'To have a friend, you must be a friend.'" Milton took it back from Spiro, folded it carefully and put it away in his wallet. "From dinner a long time ago. With Stockbridge. Still true." He looked at Spiro. "True here, too." Milton leaned back against the banquette and stared at Spiro. Milton said, "Time to go." He paused. "Both of us. Go home. Get on with it. This. All of this. You see?"

Spiro sighed, reached down for his shoes and socks, grunting from the effort. "Yes, Milton. I see." He socked and shoed himself, allowed Milton to lead him off the ship and away from the Lake, looking over his shoulder only once at the black seductive water.

Saved for now, thought Milton. Small thing. Small. It's a small thing. Leading Spiro toward the planetarium and taxis, Milton thought, but this one time, this one time, he might have done it *right*.

Every man's right.

Thirty-three

As he'd aged, no, ma*tured*, as he got *better*, har, har, har, not *older*, ow, ow, ow, Rollo's bedtime regime, *his* nightly ritual for preserving his parts public and private, had lengthened. He taped a goddamn check list to the wall over his dresser in case his memory shorted out.

To brushing his teeth, he added flossing, and then gargling with a fluoride mouthwash. Yet wait, he had to suck down his Midlife Crisis, but he wasn't supposed to drink or eat for half an hour after grutching with the mouthwash, if he followed the instructions on the bottle.

And he had to work his two aspirins in there, his vaso-dilators, or anticoagulants, or whatever the hell they were. No heart attack for Rollo, no sir.

And there were the 500 milligrams of vitamin C, chewable sour-cherry flavor. There was sugar — *sugar*, not an artificial sweetener — in the tablet.

And his allergy spray, too. He had to blow his nose before spraying, so only the nasty spray went down his throat or esophagus when he inhaled.

So. Blow nose gently, incline head backward, inhale spray dosage once in each nostril, throw down two aspirin, wash *out* taste of the spray and wash *down* aspirin with a Midlife Crisis. Chew vitamin C tablet, floss *out* sugary remnants of the tablet, brush teeth, rinse mouth with water, and grutch with mouthwash for one entire minute of his rapidly vanishing supply of them. Take that last pee before bedtime and head toward the bedroom. Brake. Go back three spaces, apply a fingertip of 1.0% hydrocortisone ointment to a fine and private place, where an unanointed itch invariably made its maddening presence known at 2:00 a.m..

Blow, snort, swallow, drink, chew, floss, brush, rinse, grutch, piss, flush, daub, yikes!

Then and only then did Rollo surrender to bed, turn on the night light and read the funnies before passing out next to his spouse, asleep but inexplicably humming on her every exhale. She dreamt recurrently of Brahms, attending a reception in his honor.

Rollo only read funny stuff before bed. Nothing sad, dramatic or even informative. Funny stuff took his mind off the carnage and cupidity at work. Funny stuff was *wise*. If he thought about work in bed, his chances of a useful erection shrank, as it were, as well as the amount of time in which he could put it to good effect.

Rollo settled in and down, but the damn dog started barking. Sharp "*Hey, shmuck!*" reports from the back porch, which his wife called "the deck," which he rejected as misrepresentation of a surface so small, decrepit, and landlocked.

"Shit," muttered Rollo. The dog, too, had *her* rituals, and she expected Rollo to respect them. He'd forgotten to bring in the beast and tender the nightly biscuit treat, so she could scramble upstairs, claws clicking on the bare oak stairs, to hide under one of the girls' beds.

With a groan, Detective Feinberg rolled out of bed, padded downstairs, let the dog in, fed her a biscuit, and let the dog *out*, because she unexpectedly insisted on it by banging her snout into his unprotected, unprepared crotch.

While he waited by the back door for the dog to demand entry again, the phone rang. He grabbed at it quickly, to shield his sleeping family from its ring. With the caution of all cops everywhere called at home in the middle of the night, he warily said only, "Yeah?"

"Detective Feinberg? This is Milton Blauser — "

"How'd you get my home number?"

There was a silence. Then Milton said, "I needed it."

Rollo said, "Excuse me. I didn't ask you why you got it. I asked you how you got it."

Another silence, then Blauser said, "Mr. McDowell — "

"*He* gave it to you?" interrupted Feinberg.

"No, no, no." Milton paused, wondering why *everyone* except Lynette was always slower than he hoped. Lynette was the only one who ever kept up with him, every time, all the time. "He's here," Milton said, "to show me a draft of his story about me. Here at Athena's Arms. Spiro is going to read it, too."

Agnew's dead, thought Feinberg, but all he said was "Ah."

"Can you come now?"

"I'm not coming. Not now. It's, Jesus, after midnight. Twelve-oh-six a.m.. I got a six-two shift tomorrow. Today."

"You aren't interested in your friend's work."

"He's not my friend," Rollo replied sharply enough to cut Milton. "I got a *life*, counselor. McDowell isn't in it. *You* aren't. My kids're asleep and that's the way I want it. Sleeping kids, sleeping wife, sleeping me. Outside in my yard, excuse me, the *bank's* yard, my dog's taking a crap, which I have to find in the morning. Nobody else'll do it. Every day, I have to pick up her crap."

"But not mine."

"Correct! I say you got 70 million bucks. You say you don't. You don't need me."

"I do."

"No, you don't," Feinberg shot back again. "Guess what? I officially retire in twenty-three hours and 54 minutes. Not that I'm counting. And I'm off the case. I found McDowell for you. You're made for each other. What is it, kismet."

But guilt — Rollo's ethnic birthright — leaked into the perimeter of his consciousness. Okay, Rollo conceded to himself, but *only* to himself, he might be Pontius Pilate on this one, might be the Judas goat — why did Christianity have all these betrayal metaphors? what the hell kind of religion needs them? — but so what? In Rollo's work, the perfect clarity of a crime, any crime, the criminal *act*, was always ruined by the cops and criminals and victims and witnesses and judges and juries crashing into each other, pissing on the chalkmarks, pocketing crime-scene souvenirs, raising needless boring questions, giving incredibly stupid answers, and thundering off on pointless tangents. He didn't need to sort it all out anymore, didn't need to prove he was superior to the people who gave him orders and the people he arrested on those orders. He didn't need to be a hero in the middle of the night for Milton.

"Detective Feinberg — "

"No magic songs. You want it your way, go for it. Live with it. G'night." Rollo hung up the phone then, but stared down at it, expecting it to ring again, to deliver another plea from Milton.

The dog's barking saved Feinberg from further irritation. Gratefully, Rollo let her in, patted her head, and followed her furry shanks upstairs.

Soundlessly, he entered the room of his first-born-by-two

minutes-daughter. She was sleeping, or feigning sleep to be left alone. He leaned down over her, kissed her on the cheek and whispered "I love you." He repeated this rite with his second-born in her room, who stirred and rolled on her side away from him.

After his nocturnal pledges of fidelity, Rollo felt calmer. Safer. But, he reminded himself, he was a fool for love. His daughters knew it, too, as they slouched on into womanhood. Boys were calling them hourly, and his girls were taking the calls. Operators, even, were standing by.

Rollo lay back down. Before he had time to arouse himself, or his wife, his conscience shifted into Park and he fell asleep. His unconscious chewed on this, though: which the hell "friend" was Milton talking about?

Thirty-Four

In Athena's Arms, having reached the end of the road with Feinberg, Milton muttered, "Such bad money. No good in it." He turned to McDowell and Spiro, seated with him at the table by the kitchen. Around them, busboys upended chairs and put them on other tables, swept and scraped and mopped, laughing and teasing each other in Spanish.

"No luck, huh?" said McDowell, through a mouthful of *baklava*. After brushing pistachio bits — most of them — from his shirt, he handed round copies of his draft. Spiro pulled reading glasses out of his shirt pocket and began to read. "We'll give him an autographed copy," McDowell said, "framed, when we move it."

"Give it away," muttered Milton, staring down at the table.

McDowell bristled. "No way. I don't give away my work."

"Not the story," said Milton. "Not the story."

"The money," said Spiro. "We have talked. It is a curse."

"Poison," said Milton, nodding.

McDowell frowned. "You guys're fucking with the plan here." He thought. Brightened. "But I like it. 'Needs thousands, gives away millions.' It's good." Fucking nuts, Pontiac thought, these two are completely unhinged, but he said only, "Yeah, we can deal with it." He looked down at the draft, skimmed it. "Here, maybe." He penciled an asterisk in the lead paragraph of his draft. "And here."

"The Nazis," Milton said.

"Pardon?" said McDowell, preoccupied with his lead.

"And the Klan."

Spiro looked alarmed.

Focusing on Milton, Pontiac asked, "What about them?"

"You can get me a list?" asked Milton, warming to his subject, eyes glowing.

"You should not do this, Milton," objected Spiro. "This is not what we said. This is wrong."

"Poison," said Milton. "The money will kill them."

Looking, no, *staring*, at Milton Blauser, eyebrows raised right up to his hairline, Pontiac McDowell said, "You're talking rewrite here. A *major* fucking overhaul."

"You can do it," said Milton.

"Yes," said McDowell, "I can." His dormant sense of shame stirred fitfully, but the story spiked it, as every story did. "And I will."

Thirty-five

The letter to Perry from the chairman of the A.R.D.C. was mild in tone, but unambiguous. The investigator assigned to the Blauser complaint had reviewed Stockbridge's submissions and met with Mr. Blauser. The investigator had no reason to pursue the matter further, in light of Mr. Blauser's satisfactory explanation of his conduct. The investigator would hold the file open for 30 days, however, pending receipt of Mr. Blauser's written response, if any. Of course, Mr. Stockbridge could reply thereto, and bring any additional information to the investigator's attention. Barring new information from Mr. Stockbridge, however, the investigator intended to close the file.

As Stockbridge considered having Milton beheaded — a *bold* stroke that just might make the difference in the Larger Scheme of Things, his secretary knocked and entered. "Mr. Brooks is here for his 2 o'clock." Perry asked her to bring Todd in.

Todd appeared behind Carmody's shoulder. He edged around her, slinking into the room like a dog pretending the vomit on the carpet wasn't his.

Appreciating Brooks's canine mien, Perry peremptorily said "Sit," and Todd did.

My client in the Thorn and Texas acquisition ... " he stopped, reminded himself of Todd's obsession with inclusion, and amended that to "our client." Todd's rocket rush of gratitude nearly blew his head off his shoulders, " ... is a foundation. My late wife's. It gives money away," the words burned in Perry's mouth, "to ... worthy causes. Scholarships for poor children, medical research, artists. I am the sole trustee — "

What a surprise, thought Todd.

"From time to time, opportunities appear, opportunities to build the foundation's principal. It is my duty, my fiduciary duty, to examine these carefully and, when appropriate, exploit them."

Like illegal immigrants, thought Todd, and sweatshop labor, nodding rapidly, hoping this oblique narrative concluded in his continued employment at D&W.

"Thorn and Texas presents such an opportunity. It is debt-free and has been soundly managed."

"And Blauser doesn't want it," Todd interjected eagerly. "It's abandoned property, essentially."

Neutrally, Perry said, "Well, that's an issue. He cares for it, but not about it. In any event, I found it, my client should have it, and my client will have it. And thank you for the memorandum on abandonment. Most interesting." Perry had filed Todd's unsolicited, elementary, *pedestrian* advisory with the three exceedingly dull but exhaustively detailed analyses of Illinois property law he'd commissioned from law-school professors. Three scholarly analyses culminating in three mutually exclusive, entirely *useless* conclusions that canceled each other out: "yes," "no," "maybe so."

"I have a temporary assignment for you, in one of our branch offices in Indiana. You're admitted there."

Indiana, thought Todd. Christ! The place exists only to keep Ohio and Illinois from crashing into each other, rubbing each other raw. Wait a minute, oh no, oh, shit, there's an office in --

" — Gary," said Stockbridge. "You'll mind it until the partner returns from rehabilitation ... "

Don't tell me why he's in rehab, prayed Todd. Please, not now.

" ... be in charge, handle all appearances, client communications as needed, for the week. You'll stay in a motel there to obviate commuting. Your salary will be adjusted temporarily, to reflect the additional responsibility." Perry studied Todd's expression. "Any questions?"

The thought, no, the *stink* of blast furnaces, refineries, slag heaps, gas exhaust stacks, the urban death rattle of endless coal trains rolling past, through, block upon block, square *miles*, of abandoned decaying buildings, rushed in on Todd. With difficulty, he focused, showed the flag. "Uh, my work, what about my work? Thorn and Texas, my other cases?"

"You'll attend to them as needed." Perry stood, signaling the end of the interview. "Mrs. Carmody has all the information you need. Keys, schedules, client matter summaries. Call her when you arrive."

Perry escorted Todd to the door, shook hands with him. At her desk, Mrs. Carmody handed Todd a building security pass, a key-card, and a manilla folder. "The motel has a 24-hour toast bar," she said, to buck him up. "All you can eat." Walking down the hall, Todd leafed through the folder, seeing nothing, hearing nothing, understanding nothing.

Next morning, in the rental agency parking lot, Todd threw his briefcase and suitbag into the back seat of the car hired to carry him to, carry him to, come on, come on, say it, to Gary. He took a deep breath and adjusted the windshield mirror. "View it as a test, Toddie," he told his skeptical, sallow reflection, which *hated* being called Toddie and suspected it was going into exile. "A test of your commitment to the firm. And the firm's commitment to you. Not exile. *Not* exile."

Todd started the car, turned west on Madison, headed over the Kennedy and drove south to the Skyway exit. He followed the Skyway to the Indiana Tollway and rode along it until the twin domes of Gary's city hall and federal building appeared on his right and the steel mills flanked the other side of the expressway to the north. A shuttered Holiday Inn smog-scraper, eroding in the acid morning mist, rose up behind the easternmost dome, windows dark and gaping. God alone knew what went on in there at night, or even during the day, and God, fortunately, didn't care to ruin Todd's day by sharing.

Todd parked the car in an open parking lot across from an office building, one of the handful of tenanted buildings in downtown Gary. He walked into the unpopulated lobby, showed his pass to the guard, rode the elevator to his office.

The front door was locked. He slipped his key-card into the slot. To his dismay or relief but Todd didn't know which, it worked. There was an outer reception area for his secretary, who was unaccountably absent. In the inner office, he settled himself behind the partner's desk. He read his work schedule for the week. He had three appearances in federal court and two appearances in state court. All were status calls for agreed continuances pending the partner's return. Light duty.

Todd switched on the partner's computer. It demanded a password. He punched his in. The computer denied him entry. He looked in the file, found the partner's password, punched it in. He was denied entry, again. "Shit," he muttered. He picked up the phone to call Carmody, but the phone was dead. The socket at the baseboard had been carefully disassembled; parts appeared to be missing. He walked out to call from the secretary's desk, but the socket there, too, was stripped of certain screws and wires.

These were careful decommissionings, preserving the form, but not the function, of the sockets.

Todd stepped out of the office into the hallway. He walked along the corridor, looking for another tenant with a phone, but there weren't any. All of the other offices were vacant, unfurnished. He rode the elevator down to the lobby, used the guard's phone and his long-distance card to call Mrs. Carmody. He explained the situation to her and she promised to send MIS and phone persons out as soon as possible. She had no idea where his secretary was but would arrange the provision of a temporary.

He rode back up to his office. With no work, he could, what? Well, he could write. By hand, on paper.

But the partner's desk was locked. The secretary's desk was locked. The file cabinets were locked. The supplies cabinet was unlocked, but cleaned out.

No legal pads. No memorandum pads. No message pads. Hell, no sanitary pads.

Todd extracted his pocket recorder from his briefcase. Its batteries were dead, and he had no replacements. Sighing, he rode down to the lobby again and called Carmody again. She wondered aloud where everything had gone and promised to get him keys and supplies as soon as she could. She told him to call the police, which he did. They came, they saw, they asked obvious questions. He gave obvious answers: most of them were "I don't know." They wrote a report, gave him a copy, and left.

After they left, sitting again at his desk, on the cover of the file jacket that contained his instructions, in the upper left hand-corner of the jacket, Todd wrote:

Napoleon in Gary, a hemorrhoid on hell's asshole.

Todd could not imagine a worse thing. Well, he could, actually, but he didn't want to: if he didn't feed the monster, he couldn't pay the bills.

Taking the light-bulb approach to creative composition, he waited for another particle/wave to shoot through his cortex. Later, *much* later, in the coffee shop in the motel, six pieces of warm whole wheat toast with raspberry jam tucked glutinously in his gut, he wrote,

'All you can eat,' Toddie. All. You. Can. Eat.

Recalling his writing instructor's writing instructions, Todd added,

Not, 'All that can be eaten, Toddie, by you.'

Thirty-six

McDowell invited Rollo to the photo opportunity over the phone the next morning. "Come on. Bring your brownie. Be a part of history."

Rollo said, "It cranks your starter, not mine. Besides, I got stuff to do. Last-day stuff."

"The gold watch and cake, right? I bet somebody'll do a fucking top ten list. You really give a shit off the record?"

Rollo thought about it before answering, slowly. "Let's see. I didn't go to Viet Nam. Never shot anybody. Well, not dead. Solved some shit now and then. Now I can laugh about it. Yeah," said Rollo certainly, "I do give a shit off the record. I love my job. You should be so lucky."

"Fuck that. I hope I die writing. Uncle Miltie wants you there tomorrow."

"He's not my uncle. And I don't see a claim check back here." Rollo squinted, trying to decipher the night shift's illegible crumpled phone messages strewn like autumn leaves on the desk before him.

"He's dropping four large on the Nazis. Four really large. Four million dollars."

Rollo lost interest in the messages. "Say again?"

"The PNSA. The Prairie National Socialist Alliance. Frank Geiss, *Obergruppen* fuckwad *Fuhrer*. The ceremony's noon tomorrow, down in front of Milton's place. They'll be waving pictures of Shitler and sieg heiling for me and my camcorder. And I expect a pantload of anti-semitic filth to beat the fucking band. What I want to know is why's it all these pisshole crackerbox fascists look *exactly* alike? You know what I mean? I mean, it's astounding. Geiss's a dead ringer for the moron who fucked up my car in Cornhole, Nebraska last summer. You remember? Off I-80? Broke off the fucking plugs when he tried to pull them with a wrench? I told you about him. Geiss's got the same stringy little mustache? The same greasy mouse-brown hair lying lank over his collar — "

"Shut up, Pontiac."

"Blauser's fucking deranged, Rollo."

"Well, you can stop it."

Evenly, Pontiac said, "No, I can't. It's not my job."

"You can stop it if you want to."

"You don't understand. It's not my job to fuck up a story. It's never my job to fuck up a story. I shouldn't even be telling you because you *can* fuck up my story." Pontiac didn't say that adding Rollo to the mix might juice the tale he wanted to tell.

Rollo said, "This was your idea, wasn't it?"

"No," said McDowell. "Let's be very clear on this, my friend. I didn't even suggest it. First off, that's making the news. Rule number one's I don't make news. Notice I am not saying fuck anywhere in here because I'm serious about this. The money's from the late Lynette Stockbridge. And there's an explanation that goes with this. You want it?"

"Yes," Feinberg admitted slowly, "I guess I do."

"So be there at noon. He won't tell me unless you're there. *Ciao!*"

Feinberg managed to shout the first two syllables of "You bastard!" into the phone before the dial tone kicked back in.

Thirty-seven

On his eleventh birthday, Carl Stockbridge was five feet, four inches tall. Just *exactly* tall enough to reach the keys on Lynette's dresser and the pedals of Perry's Jaguar XKE, and to slalom 300 feet in it, among 200-year old oaks, into the nearest neighbor's living room conversation pit. Lynette called Perry, and Perry called Milton.

Perry asked, "Can you resolve this?"

Milton said, "I'll talk to your neighbor."

"It's gotten past that," Perry said, grimly. You'll have to talk to his lawyer. He's threatening to file suit and press juvenile charges." For a moment, Perry looked lost, shook his head. "I don't understand this. He's a good boy."

After brief, intensive negotiations, the neighbor generously allowed that "Boys will be boys," and pocketed the Stockbridges' cashier's check for $218,000. "Good thing the kid was wearing a seatbelt." The smirking neighbor's subsequent trenching of his lawn and mazing of his driveway turned out to be unnecessary as well as ugly, because Carl never invaded again.

But, at twelve, Carl was expelled from his private school after picking the lock on his parents' wine cellar, stealing a bottle of 1978 Sonoma cabernet — a bit before its time — hot-wiring the football team's van, and sinking it at the deep end of the Olympic-sized pool on the school campus. At Milton's behest, the school refrained from pressing charges after full restitution and then some: Carl had to enroll in a military academy, in another state.

On the night Carl arrived home for his second Thanksgiving vacation from the academy, Lynette congratulated him on his straight-A average, rubbed his brushcut, and kissed him good night. Five hours later, she and Perry sat on a hard wooden bench in the village police station. Outside in the back seat of Perry's second Jaguar, Carl slept against Milton's shoulder.

The police station's bench was a scarred sibling to five superannuated pews resettled in the meditation garden of the village's First Episcopal Church. Upon them for forty-five years, members of the congregation had dozed or gossiped or sipped tea at wedding receptions, until Carl reduced them to kindling that night with a small but powerful homemade bomb.

"There is a pattern here, Mrs. Stockbridge." The fat and fatuous presiding cleric of the First whispered the obvious to Lynette, as he always did, which was why she'd ignored him since she was a child. "He must be seen to. The boy's at risk." Milton persuaded him, too, to forego juvenile charges.

The Stockbridges found a therapist for Carl. At the therapist's request, Carl first went by himself. Then his mother joined him. And Perry attended too, for a time. "I understand, Lynette," said Perry, "I see the issue. I will be there for you."

"And for him, Perry. For Carl."

During Carl's course of therapy, cocaine became the drug of choice among commodities brokers. While they were crashing and burning on Rush Street, down on Testosterone Row, their stashes were easy pickings for Carl. He collected them and consumed them, or cut them and sold them to former classmates, but one of them was a state police informant.

Carl was hospitalized as a condition of probation. Thanks to Milton, again.

Carl stayed clean then, for two years. To reward him, Lynette and Perry gave him a car on his seventeenth birthday, the quick red sports car that Carl embedded in an oak on Oak Street. Milton arrived at the jail without delay, but too late to bond out Carl. On hearing the news, Lynette suffered a stroke and, on Perry's instructions, died.

Remember? Milton did.

He remembered at Lynette's funeral, during the minute of silent graveside reflection the right reverend asked of the mourners before his sermon. In that minute, Milton reviewed the unbroken string of victories he engineered for the Stockbridge family. He arrived on time, on demand, in each of Carl's previous crises. He'd been the perfect advocate every time, taking full advantage of the facts and law.

Carl's downward spiral might have stopped if Milton had been too late or too early even once, or less artful. Lynette might have lived. The world might be a better place if Milton were incompetent. No, *would* be a better place, for Milton.

After the funeral, Perry returned to the office, threw himself into his work, hardened himself to his loss, set it aside. He had a firm to run, he reminded himself, the firm he built for Lynette. The practice was his monument to her faith in him. Perhaps this wasn't the best way to mourn her, but it was his way.

Milton, on the other hand, withdrew from work. Recoiled from it. At first, Perry assumed Milton was unhorsed temporarily by grief, as he was himself. He urged Milton to go away and rest, then to snap out of it. But clients complained, and Perry quarantined him.

On a cold clear evening in October three months after the two deaths, Perry strode into Milton's office. Milton looked up at him, blankly. Perry said, "I've lost my wife and son. I won't lose my practice." He turned to leave, but stopped. "You did nothing wrong. Do you understand that? I'm going over to Danville & Williamston. You can join me if you come to your senses."

Milton did not come to his senses. He had no senses to which he could come. He was whom he should be: the perfect failure. He could not *be* a better failure.

When the landlord evicted Milton from the deserted offices of Stockbridge and Blauser, Blauser took a small inheritance from an aunt and bought his building on west Madison. He relied in no way, for no purpose, on the gift from Lynette. He tended to it because she asked him to, like the houseplants of an absent neighbor. As long as he left it alone, there was no danger from it. When Perry tried to seize his dead wife's gift for her foundation, Milton foresaw the damage it would do. It had to be dissipated, destroyed.

"It has to be," said Milton urgently, on the crazed sidewalk in front of his crumbling building.

Rollo said mildly, "It's just a lot of money, Milton."

Pontiac swung his digital camcorder away from Milton and Rollo at this moment. He pointed it at the light blue Streets and Sanitation panel van pulling up and parking across the street from Milton's building. City employees in luminescent safety vests unloaded 15 sawhorses from the truck and set them in the gutter along the opposite sidewalk. Two armored police vans pulled up along the line of the sawhorses, unloaded fourteen patrolman wearing helmets and Kevlar vests. They took up positions along the sawhorses. Four squadrols drove up slowly in convoy, container-backed pick-ups each ready and able to transport eight arrestees handcuffed to benches. Two squadrols parked at each end of Milton's block, bubble lights flashing, making it impossible for cars to pass without permission. Jack McCarthy, a uniformed lieutenant from Rollo's station house, got out of an unmarked car and, flanked by two burly sergeants, strolled across the street to join Pontiac, Rollo and Milton.

Places everybody, thought Pontiac. Time to hit your marks.

The lieutenant nodded in Feinberg's direction. "Rollo."

"Jack," said Rollo. "You got this? My condolences."

Lieutenant McCarthy shrugged. "That was a nice party."

"Was there a top ten list?" asked McDowell. Lieutenant McCarthy looked at him sourly and asked, "Off the record, McDowell?"

"Yeah?" said Pontiac.

"Up yours."

"I get to stay here, Lieutenant," said McDowell. "I got an exclusive with Mr. Blauser."

"Who're you? Boswell?" asked the lieutenant, who knew his English lexicographical history from an evening city-college course. He turned to Milton and said, "You're Blauser."

"Yes." said Milton.

"Here's the deal, friend. The garbage'll be here in a couple a minutes. We bring them in. You give them the money. They do their thing. The demos do their thing over there," he nodded at the barricades across the street, "then we get the garbage out of here and the demos go away." He stared down at Milton. "Got that?"

Milton said he did, so McCarthy walked back across the street, shaking his head. One of the fem-dems was aiming a camcorder in his direction. Fuming, McCarthy pretended to ignore it. Oh, sure, *they* could record *him*, but *he*, oh, no, *he* could *not* record *them*. The fucking clumsy Red Squad had ruined law enforcement for his generation. Absolutely fucking *ruined* it. The lieutenant dispatched his sergeants to the opposite end of the blocks and took a position as far away from the camera-wielding demo bitch as he could, which didn't matter to the Peach; she wasn't interested in him as data anyway. She trained her camcorder on the main event, such as it was.

A rainbow of anti-fascist protesters formed up behind the barricades. The older tie-dyed colors sang "We shall Overcome" while the younger studded-leather hues chanted "Eat shit, Nazi scum!" in the interstices of the civil rights anthem.

Sandwiched between two more slow-moving marked cars, a dirty white battered station wagon arrived at the east end of the block. Loudspeakers mounted on the roof of the wagon blared "Deutschland Uber Alles."

"Don't do this," Rollo said to Milton.

Milton didn't respond. His eyes were fixed on the station wagon as it drew up next to the curb.

"I'll get you the money, Milton," Rollo said, desperately. "I promise."

Milton looked at him hopefully then. "Before the redemption period expires?"

Rollo said, "I don't know. I'll try."

"You aren't certain you can do it," said Milton, sadly shaking his head. He turned away from Rollo.

Anxious not to be mistaken for a Nazi, Rollo quickly walked across the street. He played to the cheap seats, standing near the policemen by the sawhorses and sneering at the fascists as obviously as he could while they emerged from their station wagon.

The Prairie National Socialist Alliance was Frank Geiss, his two younger brothers Ralph and Leon, and Leon's girlfriend Tiffany (Tiffany!). They all wore black boots, khaki slacks, and tight brown shirts — on Tiffany, the outfit was *fetchingly* tight, Pontiac noticed, thanks to weight of a big shoulder bag that pulled at her shirt. Frank carried a book-sized package wrapped in brown butcher paper.

With smooth movements born of years of practice as roadies for racial purity, Leon and Ralph set up a microphone stand, two waist-high amplifier-speakers, and corded them all together. Behind the mike stand, they set up two free standing poles, ran a clothesline from one pole to the other. They unfurled a swastika banner and suspended it between the two poles, to form a backdrop behind the microphone. Leon sound-checked the mike with a few "Heil Hitlers!" that spurred the demos across the street into fist-shaking, bird-flipping frenzy. Leon and Ralph then took up positions on either side of the microphone, arms folded across their sunken *ubermenschen* chests.

Tiffany unfolded a little canvas stool and set it up in the street. From her shoulder bag, she pulled out still another camcorder, loaded it and panned across the Geiss brothers. Then, she took a position in front of the microphone, sitting on the stool, so she could shoot up at Milton and Frank to make them look taller.

Fuhrer Frank, meanwhile, was trying to make small talk with Milton and failing miserably. "So," he said, "this is really great, Mr. Blauser. We really need this, you know? I mean, we really need it. We got big plans. And debts, you know? And wait a minute, we got something for you too." He smiled nervously, rubbing makeup onto a bright new pimple on his nose. "It's a surprise. I mean a gift. For your gift."

Milton studied him impassively, much the way a South Seas Islander might examine a white castaway washed up on the beach, half-drowned, starving, raving in some unintelligible eighteenth-century euro-tongue. "Yes," Milton said, "my gift."

"Where the hell's the TV?" whined Frank.

"I'm here," said Pontiac. He waved his camcorder. "I'm the media. Medium." Across the street, the Peach read his lips and approved his grammar.

Ignoring Pontiac, Frank said, "They're supposed to be here by now." To Leon, Frank said, "You called them, right?" To Milton, Frank said, "Leon's the Minister of Information."

"Yeah," said Leon, "I called."

"You said today, right? Noon?"

"Yeah. Noon today."

Frank craned his neck to try to see past the squadrols down the street. "Well, where the hell are they? Wait a minute, there they are." Five panel vans with extendable transmitter towers edged around the squadrols. They were painted with large station logos and pithy network-news punch-lines tested and re-tested in heartland focus groups. Invigorated by the fourth estate's advancing column, the demonstrators screamed themselves to the edge of hyperventilation.

There was the standard interval while the electronic media set up, secured their sight lines, checked their lighting, cleared their collective throat, checked *their* sound, and tested their satellite feeds. When they were ready for him, Fuhrer Frank shuffled into position behind the mike and waved Milton over next to him. Behind his hand, he whispered, "You go first, or me?"

"After you," said Milton politely.

"Great, said Frank, rubbing his hands together. "Well, this'll fuck up the kikes across the street."

Frank stepped up to the microphone, threw his head back. "Heil Hitler!" he barked. "Mr. Blauser here, he's giving us four million dollars. For our work. God's work!" he shouted at the crowd howling at him across the street. He remembered the plaque in his hands then, ripped off the wrapping paper. "This plaque is for Mr. Blauser. It says," he squinted down at it, "'Aryans Rule' and 'The Fourth Reich is Coming.' And it's got the date on it, today's date, and the amount of the money. Thank you, Mr. Milton Blauser," he ended, and edged away from the microphone. Then he hopped sideways back to it and said, "Sieg Heil!" and threw up the stiff-armed salute. The demonstrators across the street boiled and roiled in a rage for fascist blood.

Milton pulled a crumpled envelope from his left pants pocket. He walked over to Frank and handed him the envelope. Frank looked into it. He looked up, eyes wide, gave Ralph a thumbs-up. He handed the envelope to Leon and awkwardly hugged Milton, who kept his arms stiffly at his side. Then Frank turned Milton so that Tiffany could take their picture. Milton leaned into the microphone, tapped it, looked over at Fuhrer Frank. Grinning, Frank nodded and waved him on.

Looking at Frank, then at the demonstrators across the street, then back again at Frank, leaning into the microphone close enough to cause feedback, Milton said, "The police lieutenant said you were garbage." Misapprehending the subject of Milton's indefinite pronoun and ambiguous body language, the demonstrators cursed the lieutenant and the lieutenant cursed Milton. His sergeants converging from the corners, Lieutenant McCarthy ran across the street toward Milton, preparing to arrest the little bastard for the first felony that came to mind.

I retired yesterday, thought Rollo wonderingly, but he

lemminged after his former colleagues, a slave to the habit of public service.

"The lieutenant is right. You are garbage." Drawing near to mob-hood, the demonstrators surged against the sawhorses and the cops in front of them. Milton quickly turned and pulled down the banner behind him, spitting on it before Frank and Leon and Ralph could process these dissonant data. "The money will destroy you!" he shouted at Frank.

Enraged by Milton's blasphemy, the Nazi boys launched themselves at him. Rollo, Lieutenant McCarthy, and the two sergeants converged on Milton too, at that moment.

In the ensuing riot, Pontiac had the best camera angle, from the high ground of the stoop of Blauser's building, but the Peach's audio was cleaner. CNN bought Tiffany's tape even though it ended abruptly, no, *because* it ended abruptly, when one of the sergeants took it.

On his head.

Thirty-eight

It was weird, disorienting, for Rollo to sit in a witness chair and give Detective Pasquale Carlini, one of his former colleagues, *his* statement about the riot. Now, *Rollo* was one of the retired guys, the guys who wouldn't get any more off-duty security work unless they started their own security outfits and employed the guys on active duty.

"This is, what is it, ironic," Rollo said.

Like most things, including the purpose of the Miranda rule, irony was lost on Carlini, which is why he took orders for coffee and statements from witnesses. His typing was decent and his hearing was acute. Carlini looked over from the screen. "And then what happened?" he said, hands poised over the keyboard like a pianist's.

"I tackled him."

"Which him?"

"The Nazi. The head guy. I don't know. Frank? Yeah, Frank. So's he couldn't kick Milton any more. Milton Blauser. The little guy."

"Then what?"

"Well, I kind of held him down, so's Ed could get the cuffs on him."

"You hit him?"

"The Nazi boy?" Rollo looked up at the flaking paint on the ceiling. "Gee, I can't remember, you know? It was kind of wild in there for a minute or two. I don't think so."

"He hit you?"

"Oh, yeah, two-three times."

Lieutenant McCarthy appeared at his side, pulled up a chair and sat down. His right hand was wrapped in gauze. He rested it in his lap, palm up. "Sixteen people hospitalized, two with concussions. One of our people got her arm broke. Estrelita Gonzalez."

Rollo asked McCarthy, "Who's getting charged? Blauser?"

"We haven't decided. We like the garbage for aggravated battery. We like them a lot for that. I think your little playmate incited a riot, what with fighting words and all, but the corp counsel say's there's first amendment shit smeared all over this."

Rollo thought about objecting to the "little playmate" crack, but kept his mouth shut.

McCarthy flexed his unwrapped hand, squeezed his wrapped wrist with it. "An actual fucking riot, Rollo. A political riot. You know how long since we had a political riot?" asked McCarthy. "Jesus, I can't even remember the last one. When was it Passy, '94?"

Detective Carlini grunted "'92," and ran a spell-check on "aggravated." Carlini was good at spell-checks.

Rollo asked if Blauser was in the lock-up. McCarthy said, "No. He's at Cook County. Don't freak, Rollo. Observation. He's got a couple busted ribs, a concussion, but there's no internal bleeding. Little pissant's like silly putty." He frowned. "What the hell was that all about?"

Reading from the report on the screen, Carlini said, "He's got all this money he thinks is poison and he wants to give it to bad people he wants to destroy."

Lieutenant McCarthy looked over at Rollo for confirmation and got it in a nod. McCarthy rubbed his jaw. "He's going to do this again?"

Rollo said, "That's what he told me, before the shit hit the fan. Maybe he'll think twice."

Lieutenant McCarthy snorted. "Head cases don't even think once." McCarthy leaned toward Rollo. "Warn him, Rollo. Let him in on our little secret. I don't want this to happen again. One's an accident, two's a felony. I'll sign the complaint myself, he does this again. He wants to live around here, he doesn't do this shit."

"Is the Detective Feinberg here?"

Feinberg, McCarthy, and Carlini looked up. Spiro Vassilopoulos stood before them, holding a 9x12 manilla envelope. "Hello, Spiro," said McCarthy. "What're you doing here?"

"Ah," said Rollo, "the *Spiro*. I'm the Feinberg," and held his hand out and up to Spiro.

After a wave of permission from a wincing McCarthy, Spiro handed the envelope to Rollo. "Milton said I should give this to you if he is in trouble." Spiro looked worried. "He's in big trouble now, I think. I saw it on the TV."

Rollo took the envelope and slit it open. There was a

handwritten letter in it, attached to several pages of pre-printed forms.

Spiro said, "We did not agree to this. You must help. Help him. Milton."

Rollo read the letter with difficulty, but only partly because the handwriting was as small as the print in a book and quite as precise. Shamelessly, Lieutenant McCarthy read over his shoulder.

Dear Mr. Feinberg:

There are good days and bad days. I know this, on the good days. On the good days, I know also that I have bad days, when the past tears at me.

The ratio of good to bad days is changing, to my detriment. It is my hope, then, that if there is a bad day, a very bad day, you will accept the enclosed power of attorney to manage my affairs. I also have enclosed forms that you may execute to become an authorized signatory on my accounts. If there is to be an accounting for any purpose and I require a guardian, you are my nominee.

I hope you will accept this charge should it become necessary. If you undertake this task — and it will not be easy given my advancing deterioration — I have the utmost confidence that you will acquit yourself honorably, as you always have with me.

With best wishes,
/s/
Milton A. Blauser, Esq.

McCarthy said, "Do him a favor, Rollo. Get him out of harm's way. He's a victim. He asks for it often enough, somebody'll snuff his ass."

"An accounting for any purpose" tickled Rollo. An accounting, he wondered, of what?

Thirty-nine

That night, Milton *moved.*

Physically, he wriggled and writhed much less than on other nights, because he was leaden with painkillers, sedated and strapped to a jail-ward hospital bed by restraining belts. But electronically, as *information*, Milton was summer lightning, hot, fast and explosive.

Taking advantage of multiple audio-visual vantage points, television newsroom editors digitized their own raw tapes of the melee on Madison Street, and Pontiac's and Tiffany's (The Peach kept her tape to herself.). The editors spliced and spiced these data; added graphics, telestration, over-dubbing, and underscoring; started a looping inexpert haymaker from one point of view and landed it — ouch! — at another.

Local and network news broadcasts throughout Chicagoland snacked, no, *feasted,* on the riot, pimping for "Film at 5, 6, 9, and 10." Television and radio commentators weighed in, too, lightly or heavily, but instantly in either case: "What's with Milton Blauser? What's the story here?" Regretfully watching these while babysitting her great-grandson, Joan Sczuliewski predicted a nonplused visit from the A.R.D.C.'s General Counsel concerning the inactive status of the Blauser file.

In Gary, supine on his queen-size sagging musty motel mattress, buffeted by blow-dried gusts of meat-puppet anchor-prose, Todd morosely knew two things, knew them as certainly as he knew, well, as he knew *anything*: one, there was a movie in there somewhere, but, two, Todd had missed it. Whiffed *again.*

Not just a book, a medium on life-support in the cyclonic infoconomy, but a *movie.* Okay, maybe just a cheesy, made-for-TV, sidewalk-puddle-shallow-issue-of-the-minute movie with one flat camera angle per scene, but it didn't matter. It wouldn't say "Todd Brooks" anywhere on it, and that *did* matter. Todd wouldn't have a hand in it, *couldn't* write it, unless he was ready and willing to shit-can his law license and able to elbow Pontiac McDowell away from the trough.

The worst thing, the abso-fucking-lutely *worst* thing was the sight and sound of Pontiac, yap-yap-yapping on the screen. Mr. Eyewitness. Mr. Exclusive. "Mr. *Lucky!*" Todd screamed at the screen, beating his fists on the mattress, bouncing take-out-szechuan polystyrene platters off the bed, soy sauce splashing on the carpet. "Mister *Scoop*!!!"

Did the phone ring while Todd ranted? Yes, it did, and Todd lunged for it, knowing, *knowing* it was Pontiac. Gloating, prideful Pontiac, happy to rub it in. Did you read all about it, Toddie? Wish you were here, Toddie?

"Story's a fucking dud, Toddie" said Pontiac, mournfully.

"What? How can that be?" Todd asked, stunned into candor. "You're everywhere."

"Cash flow's not the point here. Problem's candy-ass editors won't let me shill for Blauser."

"Why not?"

"They like Stockbridge is a shit and Blauser's pathetic, but 'There was a *riot*, McDowell'," he scornfully mimicked whining editors made queasy by calls from outraged viewers. "'Innocent people got *injured*. Blauser's not *pitiable*. He's a fucking *nut*.'" McDowell spat scorn. "Fucking *cowards*!!"

Catching up and sprinting ahead, Todd said, "Blauser'll lose his building." A spark of, what?, *design?* flared in Todd's gut. He felt it. It was negligible but notable, casting its glow on the underside of a tiny carbon shard at the bottom of a mighty pyramid of charcoal.

"He's meat," Pontiac agreed glumly.

"What next?" Holding his breath, Todd expected to hear "agent," "publisher," or, worst, "producer."

"Fucking Thirty's next. I got a rotator-cuff condition from beating dead horses. I won't be aggravating it on this."

There's a *window* here, thought Todd, and it's opened just a crack. Cautiously, *hope*fully, he asked, "What about the story behind the story? The events leading up to, dot, dot, dot? That's great stuff."

McDowell snorted. "A coked-up puber and a rich dead bitch? Wrong, because A, nobody's dead now who hasn't been dead for ten years. B, nobody who's dead got murdered, not even close. C, I mean, spare me. All that shit's too personal. Too fucking complicated. No legs on complexity. The only challenge here was a quick pop, getting him pity-money for his building. Blauser's *way* fucked that up. Over and out, Toddie. Life's too short to suffer fucking fools."

Lashed to the mast in Gary, Todd thought he heard a Siren sing. This *can't* be the end of it, Todd hoped, there has to be *more*.

Pontiac asked, "When're you coming back?"

"Tomorrow. I'm done here. Here in hell. We'll have a drink." Energized, he lied to drive off McDowell: "Listen, I have an early court call. I have to get some sleep."

"You still owe me. You should've told me about Blauser and Stockbridge."

Impatiently piling a second lie on the last one, Todd said, "Well, I didn't really have anything when we talked."

"Bullshit," said McDowell, and hung up.

It was that, Todd admitted to himself. The last of his bullshit, he swore. He'd scraped bottom in the bullshit barrel.

Of bullshit, Todd had eaten all he could. And of toast bars, too. He packed his suitbag, checked out of the motel to stop the meter on his credit card, and drove back to Chicago, to tend the residue of *his* design, a.s.a.p., p.d.q.. To write about Milton in his office, n. P.r. Notwithstanding Perry's rules.

Todd dumped the car in the rental agency lot at 11:14 p.m. He loped into the firm's building, handed his security-pass to the sharply blazered lobby guard and scrawled his name in the night-register. Todd looked up and held out his hand for his pass, but the guard didn't hand it back to him. The guard put a cardboard box filled with plants and photographs on the counter between them. An expensive D&W envelope was taped to the side of the box.

"Hey, man," said the guard, "don't make no trouble. Please. Okay, it's my last night. I'm gone from this shit tomorrow. Got a new job. Software sales. Just take your stuff and go. Okay?"

Todd said, "Take — ?" and shut his mouth. He cradled the box in his arms, walked slowly out of the building. He gently put the box on a planter outside the building and searched through it for papers, diskettes, any remnant, any record at all, of his private writing. He found none.

Todd felt his book, his bestseller, his dream, his *hope*, explode out of him like air from a balloon crushed under an anvil.

Pity the fool.

Forty

Laws collided, putting Milton at the epicenter of a juridical Venn diagram. The tax statutes relieved him of the title to his building. The criminal statutes menaced him for the riot. And, (oh, marginal irony!) on the strength of Milton's own letter to Rollo Feinberg, late of the City of Chicago Department of Police (that is its legal name), the detective emeritus invoked the laws of probate.

Rollo hired Vivian Rucker from the fourth largest firm on LaSalle Street, an expert in mental health and mental *ill*-health. She filed an emergency petition in the Circuit Court of Cook County, Probate Division, for a determination that Milton was incompetent, in need of a guardian, *hors de combat*.

The Circuit Court Clerk's random assignment wheel routed Rollo's petition into Judge Avery Budlong's courtroom. Judge Budlong was the Ghost of Justice Present: large, bluff, red-bearded, and chubby; self-effacing, good-humored, diligent, prepared; a fount of sound decisions when litigants required them. No one would have noticed any difference in his courtroom's ambiance if he'd put a welcome mat outside his courtroom door, installed a wet bar at the bench, set buffet trays of food on his evidence tables, donned a chef's hat and an apron telling all that "Here Comes the Judge," and mingled with a beer in one hand and a spatula in the other.

It was not legally sufficient for Judge Budlong to see and hear Milton on videotape of the riot. Those might have been aberrant moments, ephemera, reversible cross-wirings of good and goony motives. So, he ordered Milton examined, commended him temporarily to the scrutiny of doctors communicating cryptically in psychiatric hip-hop.

After that, Milton was brought before Judge Budlong, who said, "With counsel's consent, I'd like to pose a few questions to respondent." The judge looked at Rollo's lawyer, who nodded. "Thank you. Sir," the judge said to Milton, "do you know who you are?"

"Milton Armitage Blauser, your honor. Age 62, a Caucasian male and an United States citizen."

Next, Judge Budlong asked, "Do you know where you are?"

"On Earth, your honor," said Milton, "in North America, in the

United States, in Illinois, Cook County. In Chicago, in your courtroom in the Daley Civic Center, courtroom 5202, on the witness stand, in this aging, wrinkled skin. And, oh, in these nice new clothes that Mr. Feinberg procured for me." Feinberg bought Milton's interview suit, as it were, from the same tailor where Feinberg got his.

"Very comprehensive, sir," commented Judge Budlong, thinking: a bit *too*, and scrawling that in a note on the legal pad before him. "And do you know why you're here?"

"My competence is at issue, your honor."

"Well put, Mr. Blauser. Well put." Quietly, the Judge added, "And your liberty, too," so there would be no mistaking the gravity of the matter. He looked steadily down at Milton for a few seconds, then said, "And you appear here without counsel. You have declined an offer of assistance from the Public Guardian, correct?"

"Yes," said Milton.

Judge Budlong continued. "Now, as I understand the petition, you have all this money — "

"I have $25, your honor."

Strike one, Milton, thought Rollo, heavily resting his chin on the pal of his left hand, staring intently at Milton. Rollo remembered how he'd wished his dying father were younger, stronger, healthier, and how the wishing had exhausted both of them and changed nothing.

"Indulge me," the judge replied mildly. "Let us agree, *arguendo*, that you enjoy ... what can we call it? ... access? ... unconditional access, to a source of money beyond your $25. Lawful access, I understand."

"*Arguendo*," conceded Milton, nodding.

"Yet, Mr. Blauser, you are in arrears in your property tax payments. In the amount of ... do you know how much, Mr. Blauser?"

"$9,418, your honor. But I have 25 of them."

"And, the court is told," he looked down at the petition and over at Rollo, "you refused, and you still refuse, to cure the arrearage from the source of funds to which you have lawful access. Is that correct?"

"Yes, your honor."

"You could pay the entire arrearage from that source of funds?"

"No, your honor, I could not."

"And why is that, Mr. Blauser?"

"Off we go," Rollo wrote on the legal pad in front of him. He nudged Vivian Rucker, showed her the note. She nodded, tight-lipped.

And off, indeed, they went. At the end of Milton's exegesis, which consumed most of an hour, the better or worse part, depending on the listener's point of view, Judge Budlong excused Milton from the witness stand. He hushed his applauding, weeping courtroom habitues and invited Rollo's attorney to put in her case-in-chief.

Rucker put Rollo on the stand, then Joan Sczuliewski, then Spiro Vassilopoulos, then Frank Geiss, jumpy as a beaten dog. And last of all, the psychiatrists. Two of them.

After each witness testified, Judge Budlong turned to Milton and asked if he had any questions of them. Each time, Milton stood and said, "No, your honor, but thank you." Judge Budlong shrugged his shoulders, slumped back in his seat, and waved on Rollo's lawyer.

At the end of this parade, Judge Budlong recalled Milton to sweep up after it. "Now, Mr. Blauser," he said. "I've heard from you and all these witnesses. I've seen the tapes." He sighed. "There are always tapes these days, aren't there? And you've heard all these persons, too. Have you witnesses in your defense? No? Well, do you have any comments on theirs? No, again? Then I'm authorized to take this petition under advisement. Or I may tell you my thinking now. Do you have a preference, Mr. Blauser?"

"Yes, your honor. Now, please."

"Ms. Rucker?"

"Yes, your honor." She looked back at Rollo at counsel table. He nodded. Rucker said, "We're ready for your decision."

Judge Budlong sharply rapped the point of his pen on his pad twice. "Where to begin?" he asked himself aloud. He thought, then straightened up in his chair. "In our social order, it's your right to spend your money as you think fit. But soft, Mr. Blauser. Note that

I said 'order.' Your right isn't unconditional. It may not be exercised to overthrow the rightful balance in things.

"Now, really, I can't know if what happened, if that donnybrook is what you meant to cause. What you intended to result from your actions. But there's uncontroverted evidence that you're indifferent to whether it happens again. And, there's evidence, again uncontroverted, that you're indifferent to risks to your well-being." Judge Budlong paused and thought. "I'm charged to be mindful of two things. Your potential to harm yourself. Your potential to harm others. I'm sure you knew that once."

Milton looked toward Judge Budlong, but not at him. His focus ended short of the bench; it was fixed on a gray canvas hammock swinging between two trees of heaven in a sun shower, as his eight-year old hands reached up to stop its motion, reached up again to wipe the rain from his cheeks.

Judge Budlong said, "You don't care for yourself as you should, Mr. Blauser. You're worthy of your best care, whatever you think. But, *but*, I may not allow you to harm others by your wilful actions. I don't like Mr. Geiss or his ilk, but in the sense that matters in this building, he is an innocent owed the law's protection. The *law's* protection.

"Yours is not a harmless self-delusion. You're not a fat jolly man who convinces a little girl he's Santa Claus at Christmastime." Judge Budlong smiled. "Rightly or wrongly, I can't say, since he wasn't before me. But I find that you are dangerous to yourself and others who've given you no cause to harm them. That is my finding. Prepare an order, Ms. Rucker."

Rucker said, "Yes, your — "

"No!" shouted Milton, surging upright in the witness stand. He subsided into slope-shouldered silence, eyes cast down again before the bailiff moved toward. But the bailiff moved anyway, stood beside Milton, a warning in the muscles bunching in his thick forearms.

"Your guardian — that will be Mr. Feinberg — may arrange for your care. I also find that your condition does not warrant confinement at this time. However, I warn you it may come to confinement if you're unable to change your ways. Mr. Feinberg will take charge of your assets and dissolve your liabilities — "

Milton looked up at Rollo. The building's gone, thought Rollo, hopelessly. Solid gone.

" — and he will keep your accounts for you."

There's that word again, thought Feinberg, frowning, and why does it stick in my skull?

Judge Budlong said, "You may recover possession of your estate when you're ready to manage it at no unreasonable risk to others." The judge leaned toward Milton and said, almost too quietly for the court reporter to hear, "You are in the grip of an obsession, Mr. Blauser. Permit yourself to heal."

Judge Budlong rose and left the bench, the audience in the courtroom standing to see him out. Milton sat in the witness stand, head bowed, until Rollo walked over and touched his arm. The detective led Milton from the courtroom. In the corridor, disgusted reporters stalked off when Rollo refused to speak and Milton vacantly ignored them.

"I want to go home," said Milton.

"Ooh, that's going to be a *good* trick," muttered Rollo, but he led Milton out of the courthouse. As Rollo scanned Randolph Street for a cab, a fat ex-cop named Ralph Riordan in a shiny green too-tight suit, black shirt, and silver silk tie hailed him. Riordan handed Rollo an envelope, said, "It's for you," and walked off quickly. Preoccupied with minding Milton, Rollo waved the envelope to draw a cab. They climbed in. Milton drew away from him and looked out the window as they rode west on Randolph. Rollo opened the envelope from Riordan and read the order to vacate issued in the name of the land trust that redeemed the property. He cursed and put it away.

Milton smiled as their cab halted in front of his building. Milton's *former* building. The frigging land-trust's building. Rollo paid the fare. Another cab pulled up. Todd Brooks stepped out, an unlit, unwrapped cigar lodged behind his right ear. Todd was dressed in running shoes, jeans, and a black tee-shirt. "Hello, Detective Feinberg," he said, "I need a job. Know anyone who has a job and needs me to do it? I'll bet you do."

"You quit?" said Feinberg.

"*Quit?*" Todd echoed, with a touch more force than the answer comfortably bore. "No, I didn't quit. I was *fired*. For theft of D&W property. They put it, that *slander*, in my *file!*"

Rollo raised his eyebrows, so Todd added, "I didn't steal anything. Just sacrificed some electrons to a muse, to amuse. And my printer. And a little paper. Everybody does it, okay? Rat *bas*tards!" Todd shouted, startling Rollo. "Where's my exit interview? Don't I get to tell them what I think?!"

"You're losing it right here?" Rollo asked wearily. He waved at Milton. "I got one already. One's enough."

"No, no," replied Todd calming quickly, "I don't think I will. I just have to chart a new course. A new course. Out of the path of rat bastards. That won't take long. I'm a hard worker. A *good* worker. Young, healthy, unattached." He thought of Louise, ached for attachment to her, forced his attention from the ache. "A bit excitable, I admit it. But I'm learning to master my emotions. Well, most of them. Getting to know myself, too. Can't you tell? What I really need right now, excuse me, *want*, is a job." Todd stopped to breathe. "A *non*-legal job."

Rollo looked at Milton and then at the building. "How much do you charge for baby-sitting?"

Todd thought, calculated. "You only have a week here." Shrinking from Rollo's glare in response to his ill-considered reminder of the order to vacate that Todd himself had drafted while still in Gary, Todd quickly said, "Forty an hour, plus meals. Don't look at me like that. You can afford it. And I'm worth forty an hour. I can clean and drive. I know CPR and where all the best restaurants are." Todd paused, thought, decided. "Okay, full disclosure. The New Todd. I have 150K in the bank, but that's the mortgage, loans and food if I don't get work. Full disclosure? I got *fired*. The market's tight for losers. Oh, my, yes. But I need to get *paid* like I'm doing law. I still have loans. Remember loans? Biting the ass that borrows them?"

Feinberg reluctantly grunted a yes. "You'll have to stay here with him. He won't stay anywhere else." Whispering, he added, "Milton doesn't know about the order yet."

"File a motion for reconsideration," said Milton, dreamily.

"'And Tommy doesn't even know what day it is,'" Todd sang loudly, badly.

"Hey, Milton," Rollo said, "pay attention next time. I need all the help I can get." Rollo looked up at the building. "What the hell'm I going to do now?"

What, indeed, besides retaining a *second* lawyer, a property tax redemption specialist named David Whitman, to file an emergency motion for reconsideration of the order to vacate? Whitman also requested a stay of execution of the order to vacate. He sorrowfully cited the changed circumstances — a guardianship appointment — in his supporting memorandum. He forcefully argued for the need to temper customary process with consideration of sad exigencies like this, and with a little professional courtesy for a stricken colleague.

Whitman was more eloquent than Perry's partner representing the land trust, but not as well-wired. After comparing the parties' political throw-weight, Judge Arthur McGarrity, the author of the order of vacation opined, "Your motion for a stay is denied, counsel. And the motion for reconsideration, that's denied too. But it was well-argued. Really. Approach the bench." At their sidebar, McGarrity reminded the two lawyers to meet him two weeks hence at the monthly luncheon of the bar association's Real Estate Law Committee.

Rollo consulted a *third* lawyer, an appellate specialist. She reviewed the pleadings and transcripts, and estimated the odds on winning reversal of the order to vacate as way past the skinny side of zero. She sent him off with this: "There's no legal flaw in McGarrity's order and no abuse of discretion here. None I can see, anyway."

Rollo rejected the idea of betting on an imaginary number by taking an appeal. Unhappily, he made plans to move Milton's paper to a record-storage warehouse, and to move Milton himself, to "a, what is it, an undetermined location, honey," he evasively told his wife. "Just for a little while."

She saw through *that*. "Where will we put him?" she asked plaintively. "We don't have a spare bedroom, and the basement is a mess. It isn't even finished."

"It isn't?" Rollo asked.

Forty-one

Louise Melville and the Langley Peach continued to meet for their weekly squash match, even after D&W fired Todd and the Peach concluded that Louise would not tell her anything that mattered to Perry. Their matches made each of them a better player, because each believed she could win every game, but only if she played her best, only if she took the calculated risks, only if she *gambled* on the strength of cresting endorphin.

They knocked each other all over the court that morning, with brute force more evident than style. After the Peach took two out of three games, they steamed and showered and shampooed and whirlpooled and rinsed off the whirlpool's chlorine and dressed to the waist and made themselves up, minimally. They finished dressing and repaired the bar in the club, to spoon yogurt and pick at salads.

The Peach and Louise executed their customary conversation. Each sentence hid content from the listener. Indefinite nouns plodded after opaque antecedents. Fuzzy generalities flowered out of useless detail.

"There is an inevitability to things," said the Peach.

Louise accepted this as a statement of fact, rather than a disguised question.

The Peach asked, "What did you want to be when you were a girl? Young, but not too young. Old enough to think seriously about a real career."

Deciding she could safely answer this question, Louise said, "A meteorologist. I knew the names of all the clouds. Nimbus, cirrus, cumulus, stratus. The hybrids. I had a barometer and thermometer outside my bedroom window." The clouds always changed, Louise thought. She'd seen so much in them.

The Peach said, "I expected to be a prima ballerina." She smiled, allowed herself to sound wistful. "I might have been," she said.

Louise smiled, too. They chewed more greens in silence.

The Peach said, "You'll be seeing your beau."

In my nightmares, thought Louise, but she asked, "Will I?"

"You have to decide whether the man in him, the good man in him, can emerge."

"I don't have to do any such thing."

The Peach said, "You might do something about him."

Louise said, "I suppose I might."

The Peach laid her fork carefully on her plate and daubed at her lips with her napkin. "When I am trying to work a thing out, think it through, I call my mother. She is a deep sweet well of good advice." She paused. "There is a gentleman in my life. An older gentleman. He brings me ... complexity." The Peach laughed. "I sound so antebellum."

"Is there a wife?" asked Louise, amazed by this sidelong lurch into intimacy.

"Yes," said the Peach, declining the opportunity to split hairs.

"But he loves *you*," said Louise. "He swears he loves you. And he'll divorce her, he *swears* he will. But he can't do it now. He needs to *prepare* her."

"Oh, honey," said the Peach, sadly, "divorce is out of the question. But I have asked him, entreated him, to come away with me."

"So you will ... well, what will you do?"

"A prima ballerina," mused the Peach. "I got awfully close, too. I'm preparing to dance on out of town. I've never liked to cast another's shadow. Hide in them, yes, but not lose myself in them. I helped an old man feel younger again and a young woman feel older. I believe I've met all my obligations here. I've even done my good deed for the decade." She shivered. "And your autumn is coming on. Your autumn is my winter. And your winter is anathema."

"It's good for us," Louise replied. "Builds character. And it's not so hard anymore. Global warming. El Nino." Louise looked at the Peach. "I don't know what you do, but I suspect the worst."

The Peach smiled and said, "That's a bit editorial. Or is it empathic? Well, I guess this is one time I'll have to find out when everyone else does." The Peach stood up and swung her athletic bag onto her shoulder. "I'm going home for a while. Send the invitation here." She pulled out a card with a post-office box number on it.

"The invitation ... ?"

"To the wedding, dear girl, to the wedding."

Louise stood up, too, then, and extended her hand to the Peach.

The Peach pulled it gently past her and embraced Louise. They hugged and kissed each other's cheek. Louise asked the Peach if she needed a ride to the airport: "I mean, if that's how you're leaving."

"Thank you, no."

"You are so polite."

"An artifact of my upbringing."

Unpacking her gym bag at home that night, Louise found in it a compact disc mailer shrink-wrapped in plastic. On the disk inside, a line of scrawled and nearly indecipherable cursive traversed the label. Louise identified it after a moment as Todd's signature.

There was leaf of cream-colored stationery in the mailer, too. She unfolded it and read this typed sentence centered below the fold:

The suppression of art is always a greater wrong than any theft that enabled its expression.

Louise lifted the sheet of stationery to her nose. There was a faint but unmistakable fragrance of peach.

Forty-two

Bananas worked in Rollo's Midlife Crisis. Strawberries worked. Crushed ice was stellar, crushed ice from spring water.

Prune juice did *not* work. Prune juice was overkill. Gutwrenching overkill.

The formula for Rollo's elixir of regularity was stabilizing after innumerable hit-or-miss experiments, which was good, because, Rollo said, "Nothing else is. Everything else is a frigging mess." Rollo stared gloomily into his drink at the bar in Athena's Arms. He looked up and nodded at two TAC officers in baseball caps and kevlar vests as Heidi led them to their table for lunch. They nodded back, but just barely. The TACOs' eyes shifted away from Rollo, back to Heidi's brave vibration each way free; they didn't want to recognize a pensioner. Pensioners frightened them more than gangbangers. Kevlar couldn't protect them against time.

Pontiac was incredulous. "You don't like running all that money?"

Rollo shook his head. "I don't sleep nights. I got no time to study for the bar. My girls are hocking on me. We can't go canoeing because I can't leave Milton — "

"Take a cellular. No. A satellite phone. You can go anywhere. Downlinks're the end of privacy. No man's an island."

Oblivious to the white noise emerging from Pontiac, Rollo continued with " — it's who makes the decisions." Rollo poked the bar top with a finger. "I mean investment decisions, hour-by-hour, minute-by-minute." Rollo waved his arms above the bar, like a trader on the floor of some frantic stock exchange. "Buy! Sell! Hold! Do I let him run Thorn and Texas? He made all the money, but he's nuts. There aren't any stockholders, so he runs it into the ground, he doesn't hurt anybody else. But I'm not supposed to let that happen, so do I take it out of his hands? But he made all the right decisions while he was nuts to begin with. I mean, my fiduciary *duty* here, it's chewing its own butt. And everybody except Milton wants the money. Stockbridge wants the money. Jesus, *I* want the money. It makes me *crazy* being close to all that money. And every day, I'm hiring more lawyers. Lawyers're crawling all over me. Like lice. I feel like, you know, Gulliver."

As Spiro passed their table, beating a path to the hostess station,

Pontiac called out, "Innkeeper! It's getting chilly in here. Throw another lawyer on the fire!" Pontiac sucked at his beer. Around his glass, he asked Rollo, "'How many lawyers does it take to change a light bulb?'" When Rollo didn't respond, Pontiac finished the riddle: "'How many can you afford?'"

Rollo said, "I'm paying Todd Brooks 40 bucks an hour to watch a sixty-two-year-old who doesn't even have Alzheimers. Seventy million dollars is a frigging pain in the *ass*, is what it is!!"

McDowell shrugged. "So pay yourself a fat management fee for your aggravation. Or quit. Go take care of your beautiful family."

"No," Rollo shook his head. "I don't quit. Nobody makes me quit. I'm thinking maybe I dust Milton. Or Mr. Babbling Brooks. As a public service. They yak all the time. They're like, what is it. Soul mates. Mumbling, raving, ranting, blah, blah, blah. It's disgusting. They're making me crazy, but I won't quit. No. They can't make me quit."

"Don't sweat it," said Pontiac in a soothing tone. "You're doing fine. And you're doing the *right* thing. You got the high ethical ground here." Pontiac paused, cocked his head. "Was that moral support? Like your wife cheers you up after a hard day at the office?" Pontiac thought, he *is* doing the right thing, and then thought, why did I think *that*?

Perhaps because Spiro appeared, leaned in between them, draped an arm over each shoulder. "So glad you came!!"

Pontiac said, "What?"

"That is why you are here. Because I wanted you both, no?" He clapped Rollo on the back. "This will make a difference!"

Rollo said, "No."

Spiro said, "No?"

Pontiac, said "Yes. No."

Ignoring McDowell and Spiro, Rollo added absently, "And there's a, what is it, this account thing ... "

Pontiac McDowell asked, suddenly attentive, "What 'account thing'?"

"Milton talked about an 'accounting.' In this letter he wrote me? 'If there is to be an accounting for any purpose ... ' And every time I hear the word 'account," I get this little, what is it, a jolt, you know? What's that all about?"

Spiro thought, it is time. For you, Milton. Spiro swore to himself, I will be *good*. He squeezed Pontiac's shoulder and moved away.

Watching Spiro walk off, his eyes hunting for Heidi, Pontiac thought, he's right: Rollo doesn't know. Shit, shit, *shit*! He doesn't *know*. I can raise this story from the dead. Or I can give it *away*. I can be the *hero*. Like Bob and Carl. Save the planet. I never give anything away, Pontiac reminded himself. Never. Wait! The ruling class fears disorder, chaos, the uncharted. The improbable outcome. The unpre*dic*table outcome. "How can I be anybody's nightmare?" Pontiac complained aloud. "I'm not a fucking anarchist. I'm just a neon sign. On-off, on-off. Fuck this, fuck that. You can time the fucking pulses. You can set your fucking watch by me. Fuck, fuck, fuck, oh, shit." Unable to stop himself, he said, "It's in the bag."

"Don't try to make me feel better." Rollo dug behind his left-most lower molar with a toothpick. "I mean, I don't know what I'm doing. And I don't know how to ... " He trailed off.

Pontiac belched. "Pay a little fucking attention here. I got something for you." Pontiac gambled a little and said again, "It's in the bag. The fucking *bag*." He paused. Observed. Nope. Nothing. Pearls before ... never mind. Pontiac leaned toward Rollo, said, "But I need a fucking commitment before I give it up, okay? A deal." Pontiac shook his head. "What a fucking *mor*on! Staring me in the fucking *face*!" Rollo looked offended and Pontiac said, "Not you. Don't get excited. I mean *me*. *I'm* a fucking moron."

Rollo said, "For ... ?"

"For little Milton's ass." Pontiac beamed.

Rollo thought: toads on *crack*.

Pontiac said, "I mean *saving* his ass. And his building. Here's the deal: what I tell you, no, what I *show* you, right now, you take to court. To court. Nowhere else, okay? Straight to court. Tomorrow. *O*pen court." No time for anyone else to get a piece, thought Pontiac. All mine, all mine, all *mine*. Pontiac said, "Call the fucking judge today. McGarrity. The Chancery pig, the guy that pulled the plug. Emergency motion. No private deal, no settlement. *Especially* no sealed record. Nobody's fucking face gets saved. This is fucking *public*." Pontiac gazed out the window. "'Sunlight is the best disinfectant.'"

Rollo said, "Brandeis."

Pontiac said, "It wasn't Oliver Wendell Holmes. Or Sherlock fucking Holmes, Sherlock. That's what we got here. A ray of fucking *light*." Pontiac looked over at Rollo. "Nothing unethical, buddy. I got my reputation here. What I mean is, I mean I'm a mean fucker, but I'm not *bent*, you know? It's a one-time offer. You'll fucking *love* it."

Rollo asked, "This's good? I mean, this'll work?"

Pontiac shrugged, a trick for someone with invisible shoulders. "Well, I don't know if it'll *work*. I'm not a fucking clairvoyant." Pontiac brightened. "*But*! It'll blow things up. *Up*! Can that be bad? That's *good*. Anyway at this point, what else've you got? And this'll *feel* good." Pontiac shivered with pleasure. "Face it: you're fucking tapped, anyway. What else you got?"

Rollo thought, said, "What else've I got?" He inhaled, exhaled, slowly, slowly. "Okay. Deal."

Pontiac thought, okay. In for a dime, in for a dollar. Pontiac said, "It's in ... the bag."

Rollo frowned.

Pontiac giggled. "No, man. I mean it. The yellow bag. Milton's yellow bag."

With difficulty, Rollo focused on Pontiac's face, where big flappy lips formed these words: "Milton's. Yellow. Bag. Go look. You know. The yellow fucking suit case. *Brief*case."

"His briefcase ... ?"

Pontiac said, "That's all I got. All I fucking got. The plastic fucking briefcase. Now're we going over there or what?"

Rollo drained his Crisis, started to slide off his bar stool, but Pontiac grabbed his arm. "No. Wait. Let's go get Spiro. He might come in handy. In case there's a scene or something, you know? Yeah. A scene."

They found Spiro in the kitchen, exchanging constructive criticism with his chef Dimitrios in a language that combined equal measures of Greek, Spanish, American, and — wow! — Anglo Saxon.

When Spiro and Dimitrios ran out of four-letter suggestions for improving kitchen process and outcomes and put down the carving knives each of them was waving for purely rhetorical effect, Pontiac took Spiro's arm and led him out of the kitchen. "Watch this," Pontiac said to Rollo. "Spiro. Yellow bag. You know something about Milton's yellow bag?"

Spiro smiled, but said, "I ... no. No. I don't want to say nothing."

Pontiac winked at Rollo, said, "Okay, then," and walked out into the warm August air. Going slowly to avoid breaking the sweat barrier, they strolled to Milton's former building, which they held for another two days, but no longer. Up the stairs and into Milton's apartment.

It was empty of files now; all of them were in storage. A new convertible sofa crouched and couched under the window overlooking Madison Street. Milton lay on it, staring out the window, head pillowed on his yellow bag, wiggling his fat little bare toes on the far arm of the sofa warming in the sunshine. Todd sat cross-legged on the floor, leaning against the couch, writing on a legal pad and drinking fancy coffee in a double paper cup from a fancy coffee bar. Todd looked up and said "Hey, hey," *much* too nonchalantly tucking the legal pad out of sight.

Rollo suppressed an urge to scream and asked Milton, "What's in the yellow bag?"

Milton didn't answer, but he sat up, pulled the bag out from behind his head and handed it to Rollo. Milton wormed back against the arm of the couch, laid his head on it, and closed his eyes again.

Pontiac said, "Go ahead. Look in the bag."

Rollo opened the bag, withdrew the contents. He skimmed the original partnership agreement for Stockbridge & Blauser, in a manilla file folder gone gray from unprotected aging. He read death certificates for Lynette and Carl Stockbridge.

And he opened a ledger book. On the first page, headed by a month-day-year date that matched the one on Lynette's death certificate, Rollo read a handwritten list of names. Businesses and individuals.

On the ledger's second page, headed with a date on the first of the month following that given on the first page, Feinberg saw the same list, but with one name stricken, citing to the *Chicago Tribune*, date, section, page, byline.

On each succeeding page, dated at first-of-the-month intervals, the same list, changing slowly, names appearing and disappearing and sometimes reappearing, each change with references. References to newspapers and magazines going as deeply as the author's name at times, but not always. The last marked page was dated July 1 of the year in which Rollo and Spiro and Pontiac and Todd and Milton stood and sat and reclined in that room.

Rollo looked at Milton and asked, "What's this?"

Milton opened his eyes and looked over, focused. "Client list," he said. "Incomplete. No comprehensive sources." Milton closed his eyes again, smacked his lips, began to snore.

"'No comprehensive ... ' Jesus." Rollo looked down at Todd. "You can't talk to me, but I can talk to you. This ... " he handed Todd the ledger " ... is the book on Stockbridge & Blauser. Current to this month."

Todd leafed through it. "And your point is ... ?" he asked.

Rollo said, "There are current clients of Danville & Williamston on the list. You don't have to tell me that. I know that because they're named in the frigging articles. The frigging articles," Rollo pointed at the ledger, "cited therein."

Pontiac said, "Oh, my, yes."

"They're not *my* articles," replied Todd mildly. "There's nobody and nothing in my articles. I don't have any articles. Maybe I should get some. What do you think?"

"Milton?" said Rollo, but got no immediate response. So Rollo said, it again, loudly, more loudly than he intended, and Milton awoke, rubbed his eyes. Rollo retrieved the ledger from Todd and asked Milton, "Why do you keep this list?"

"Why?" Milton asked, puzzled. He sat up.

"Because," Rollo shouted triumphantly, shaking the ledger in Milton's face, "you want it! *Want* it!!"

"Want what?" asked Todd.

Milton closed his eyes, shook his head, covered his ears. "I do *not* want it!" he shouted back, rocking on the couch.

Spiro went to sit beside Milton, put an arm around his shoulder, said, "Please. He wants to help."

To Milton, Rollo said, "Oh, yes, you do. You want it big time."
Rollo said to Todd, "He wants Stockbridge & Blauser back."

Milton said, "It's the fruit of the poisonous — "

"Don't start," said Rollo, quietly, more quietly than he intended. His volume control failed him, as it always did in crises.

Todd said, "Excuse me, but so what? What if he does want it?"

"I got leverage!" said Rollo. "I can get Stockbridge off his back."

Todd argued, "How? It's too late. He *abandoned* his interest in the firm. I researched that." A breach of attorney-client privilege loomed up spectrally over Todd. "I think I have to be quiet again."

"Fruit of the poisonous tree," moaned Milton, rocking on the couch. "Don't want it. Don't want it."

"He abandoned it?" asked Rollo. "You did all the research and you're sure, huh? Fortunately, *fortunately*, I'm the guardian here. You're the guardian, he's out on his *ass*."

"He *is* out on his ass," Todd shot back.

"You think so? All the research? You think so?" Rollo ran out the door, stuffing the ledger and death certificates in Milton's yellow bag as he headed down the steps. Stopped at the base of the steps, struck by thunder, no, by *in*sight. For a minute, he thought something *through*. "Yeah," he said to himself, nodding, "that's good, too."

Upstairs, Pontiac looked at Spiro, sitting next to Milton, who had his head in hands. Pontiac said, "Happy now? You got him what you think he needs, and look at him." Spiro didn't answer, so Pontiac said, "Oh, fuck this," and followed Rollo *out*.

Upstairs, Todd retrieved his legal pad, settled it on his lap. He sang softly to Milton, but still badly, "'You can talk to me. You can talk to me. If you're lonely you can talk to me.'" Todd waited for Milton, patiently waited for him to return from his darkness.

Forty-three

Don't ask a Jungian to parse Freud or a cop to master, *instanter*, the wafer-thin nuances of property law. Rollo knew what he was looking for but next to nothing about it. He recalled first-year property law, taught to him by a Professor Cunningham who was neither cunning nor a ham, but it could take Rollo hours, days, weeks, months to assure himself that he'd found all the nooks and crannies, dips and turns, conditions on exceptions to rules.

So Rollo paid a visit to David Whitman, the real-estate specialist he previously consulted, to acquire quick opining on an issue in property law. "The way the last deal worked out," Rollo said, "I got misgivings. Doubts. And you got ... " Rollo looked at his watch, " whoa, 19 hours."

"Thanks," Whitman said sourly. He still fumed about losing Rollo's motion to stay the order to vacate.

"I'm giving you a chance to go one-for-two for the client. Get your average out of the gutter. The guy's about to lose his home."

"With 70 mil — "

"Don't say it," Rollo warned. "Don't talk about the money. The only thing that matters to him's the frigging building, okay? His, what is it, his anchor."

Call me tomorrow morning, at nine," said Whitman. "I'll let you know how it's going."

"No," said Rollo. "Not tomorrow. We go *in* tomorrow at nine. To court. I made a deal, okay? You call me at home tonight. Whenever. Let me know how much closer I am to right or wrong. If you got the goods, write it tonight. Then we take it from there."

"You'll get a disclaimer-rich product," said Whitman.

"I can handle it," said Rollo, and left.

He arrived on time for his appointment with another specialist, in business organization, an overlapping discipline, whom he retained on the same terms. After a similar discussion, he left.

However Rollo got his research, and whatever the result, he wanted two opinions, and two angles, on its reliability.

Next he loped over to the A.R.D.C. At reception, he asked to see Joan Sczuliewski. The receptionist said, "She's in a meeting."

Rollo said, "It's urgent. *Very* urgent."

Doubtfully, the receptionist said, "I can page her."

Rollo said, "You'd be doing the right thing. Saving a life even." Noting her skeptical expression, he added, "okay. It's *like* saving a life, but it's, you know, close. Very close. A little mope, maybe, but he's entitled." Rollo felt for the comfort his badge, but remembered he didn't have it anymore.

The receptionist made one of the choices receptionists always can make at this moment: she sat up a little straighter and said, "Okay. I'll do it." Gripped by resolve, she punched a button on her console and paged Sczuliewski to come to reception. (Rollo noted the pronunciation, too, pleased he got it right.)

Rollo sat and leafed through a magazine for about a minute. Stood up again, looked over at the receptionist, slumped back into his chair.

Joan Sczuliewski walked into reception, looked around. Saw Rollo, recognized him, said, "You're ... "

Rollo stood up and said, "Feinberg. Rollo Feinberg."

She nodded. "Yes. Milton's guardian." She corrected herself: "Mr. Blauser. I saw you at the hearing."

Rollo said, right, right.

Sczuliewski said, "How is he?"

"Not good," Rollo said, "But I got something for you. A what is it, a complaint."

She smiled as little as she could, said, "And why is it so urgent?"

"It's about Milton," he said. Added hurriedly: "Not against him. A complaint for him."

Sczuliewski said, "On his behalf?"

Suddenly anxious, Rollo said, "I can make it, can't I? I'm his —"

"Guardian. Yes." She stepped aside. "Shall we go to my office?"

Rollo shook his head. "No time, no time. Look I'll just lay it out here."

And Rollo opened Milton's yellow briefcase and pulled out the client list and showed it to Sczuliewski.

And Rollo talked and pointed at lines on the client list and waved his arms and talked some more.

When he stopped, Joan Sczuliewski smiled again. This time, as much as she could. She said, "May I make a copy of that list?"

"Yeah, sure," said Rollo. "But I ... " he looked at his watch, " ... can you do it right now? I have to go. To the library. Look at some law. I mean, no, wait, go ahead. I'll wait here."

Sure, she said. And walked down the hall to the service center and copied the client list. And walked back and gave the original back to Rollo. And retreated to her office.

The entire time, Joan Sczuliewski hummed to herself.

A habit preceding — in her colleagues' experience — the laying-on of just desserts.

Forty-four

Rollo had time to kill before the close of business, before he got his two specialists' answers, so he went after all to the Cook County law library atop the Daley Center to research the same two issues. He shared space at a table between a pant's-pocket practitioner and a *pro se* paranoid receiving signals from Mars through her molars.

Rollo stayed in that public library until it closed, pulling books off shelves, marching around with stacks of them in his arms, pencil clenched piratically in his teeth. Rollo needed to know that he knew what he could know, that he'd done his homework as well as he could; not assumed, guessed, surmised, inferred, believed.

By closing-time, he knew what he knew in black and white: yes, no, maybe so.

Forty-five

At 7:48 the following morning, Perry Stockbridge received from Mrs. Carmody the news that D&W's managing partner, Langdon Danville, wanted to see him in the partner's dining room.

Perry arrived as Danville swallowed the last sterling silver spoonful of his customary soft-boiled egg and started to butter his wheat toast. Danville was the 68-year-old, first-born heir of a D&W founder and, despite that, a not entirely incompetent lawyer.

Danville patted his lips with his white cloth napkin and looked up when Perry approached him. "Ah, Perry. Thanks for joining me on such short notice. Please, have a seat. Hungry?"

"No, Langdon."

"Well, then, I'll get right to it." He cleared his throat. "Thorn & Texas. One of your matters, isn't it?"

Which Perry knew wasn't the point. Yet. He nodded. "An acquisition for a client, The Lynette Foundation. Proposed acquisition. Nearly completed."

"And it involves Milton Blauser, doesn't it?" Danville chuckled. "In some utterly obscure and clever way, I understand he owns T&T."

"He appears to own it, yes."

"And we have taken a building of his, I understand? In a tax foreclosure?"

Perry said, "What's the point here, Langdon?"

Danville blinked. "I took a call this morning." He produced a pink message slip from his jacket pocket. "From Wilbur Farrington. You know him. The Executive Director of the A.R.D. C." Danville mused. "Went to North Shore Country Day with him." He smiled at a memory. "*Terrible* lacrosse player. Well. It seems one of his investigators, Wilbur's ... "he looked down at a piece of paper at his left, " ... a Zoo, a Seezoo, oh, never mind. One of his investigators took in a complaint against us yesterday. Against the firm. And against you, personally, Perry. Concerning Blauser. And Thorn and Texas. Complainant's name is ... " relieved he could pronounce the name, " ... Feinberg. Rollo Feinberg. Hmm! 'Rollo.' An unusual name. Know anything about this?"

A lobe that managed adrenaline *pinged* in Perry's skull, but he said, "I haven't the vaguest idea."

"Well, it was all very hurried. He was on his way to a meeting, Wilbur, but he called as a courtesy. Wilbur. Before the, before the formal complaint. Is issued." Danville avoided Perry eyes, preferring to focus, not surprisingly, on Perry's left jugular. "Said something about a ... " he consulted his phone message a third time, " ... "a conflict." He looked up. "You did a conflicts check?"

Perry said, "Of course," but thought, before we knew he – .

Mrs. Carmody distracted him from the forming thought by entering the dining room with a sheaf of papers in her hand. She headed for Perry and handed them to him. "It's an emergency motion," she said. "For nine a.m., in front of Judge McGarrity."

Undeterred, Danville consulted his note one last time. "And an 'accounting' of some sort."

"Don't know anything about that," Perry said sharply. He looked down at the papers, at the caption on the Notice of Motion: "Land Trust 14178 v. 1138 West Madison." Further down, in the text of the notice, he read the title: "Emergency Motion to Reconsider Order of Vacation."

"What's that?" asked Danville.

Reconsider, thought Perry. He stood up. "I have to go." He waved the papers. "Prepare for the hearing."

Danville said. "Glad you did a conflicts check. I'm sure this is nothing. Just crackpot — "

"Yes," said Perry. "Sorry. I have to go."

Langdon Danville watched Perry leave the dining room. He took a last sip of orange juice. At a wall phone by the door of the dining room, he called the firm's ethics officer and told him to meet him in the Daley Center, in McGarrity's courtroom.

Forty-six

Any morning, the sheriff's deputies "guarding" the lobby of the Daley Center courthouse might make the lawyers heading into court play the Special Security Guessing Game. The Game goes like this: the lawyers have to guess whether the deputies will (a) direct them to stand with the hoi-polloi in the long lines leading to the metal detectors, or (b) admit the lawyers through the judges-and-lawyers-only entrance, where, feeling special, the advocates wave their A.R.D.C. cards and sheriff-issued passes and leave the clients and witnesses and crazy derelicts in their wakes. When the lawyers go through the special entrance, they don't have to take off their belts or cell phones, or empty their pockets into plastic refrigerator-left-overs boxes, like hoi-polloi everywhere there is Security these days, or the appearance of it.

The deputies especially like to direct the lawyers to line up with the bar-card-have-nots and then re-direct them immediately to the lawyers' gate, which makes no sense to anyone, but many of the deputies are only pretend law-enforcement officials anyway. Their *real* job, still, is precinct captain.

These deputies are hired despite their law-enforcement IQs, which aren't even average, because they Get Out The Vote for the Sheriff, years, *decades*, after the reported death of the Machine. They couldn't get jobs as dishwashers with the high-end private-security firms staffed with ex-Special Forces commandos, guys who actually guard things and people, but these deputies have well-shined black shoes and navy blue uniforms and guns and handcuffs, so no-one argues with them, even though putting weapons under their control makes even less sense than their herd-management practices. But, *but*, they get out the vote and that's the litmus test that matters there.

That morning, Rollo's lawyers passed through the lawyers' gate. Rollo went through the screening machines with the have-nots.

But Rollo was in the courtroom with his three-count-'em-three lawyers when Perry arrived. Stockbridge recognized David Whitman, the real estate lawyer who'd unsuccessfully moved before to stay the order of vacation, and Something-or-other-Rucker, the female lawyer who'd handled the involuntary petition for a declaration of Milton's incompetence. The third lawyer was unknown to him.

The entire Kennel trailed in Perry's wake. He glanced across at Rollo, who was, unaccountably, smiling, no, grinning, no, *smirking* at him. Perry felt ... what? Dislocation? He couldn't name the sensation, but he didn't like it. It felt like food-poisoning.

Perry motioned to his associates to sit behind him in the first row of pews, except for one acolyte, whom he ordered to join him at the bench and take notes. Perry saw, in the first row behind Rollo, the foul-mouthed Pontiac McDowell and a dark Mediterranean man. (Actually, he was Aegean, but it's a common mistake.) The dark man sat next to Louise, who had Milton on her right. Todd Brooks slumped on Milton's right side.

Perry saw Langdon Danville slip into the last row, with the firm's ethic specialist, a lawyer named Emmitt Markell.

Then Judge Arthur McGarrity entered the courtroom. A lanky, cranky older man with a permanent scowl (except for *pro se* litigants, whom he treated with flawless courtesy), he affected a sky-blue robe with ermine sleeves, after an English Chancery Lord he saw on a visit to the Inns of Court.

McGarrity's courtroom deputy said, in a single sentence, "All rise be seated, court is in session." McGarrity's clerk called out "Land Trust 14178 v. 1138 West Madison, 04 CH 55999."

Rollo's three lawyers, accompanied by Rollo, approached the bench. Perry strode toward it, too, with his scrivener. David Whitman and Perry Stockbridge each said, "Good morning, your honor."

Rollo's lawyer said, "David Whitman for movant."

"Perry Stockbridge, for respondent."

McGarrity looked out over his glasses, said, to Whitman, "You, I recognize. And you," nodding at Rollo. He indicated the other lawyers. "Who're the rest of these people?"

"Vivian Rucker, your honor. I handled Mr. Feinberg's petition for a guardianship for Mr. Feinberg. In Judge Budlong's court. I mean, for Mr. Blauser. The owner."

"Former owner, your honor," said Perry.

Rollo's third lawyer said, "Alex Brinstein, your honor."

Judge McGarrity said, "Why do I know your name?"

Brinstein said, "I think you came to an ethics seminar I ran last year. For the Circuit Court?"

"Oh, right. I remember that." He peered at Stockbridge, raised his eyebrows, said, "An ethics lawyer?"

Perry said nothing.

"Well," said McGarrity, "I have your papers, counsel. Who's going to talk first?"

Whitman said, "On behalf of movant, your honor. You have a motion to reconsider. It's pretty straightforward — "

"No it's not," complained McGarrity. "You're saying in here that the order to vacate was improperly procured. That the entire tax sale proceeding, in fact, was improper." Reading, the judge said, "'Fatally tainted by conflicts.' I see a bunch of unsupported allegations, but I don't see any factual basis for this. No affidavits. Nothing."

"Your honor," said Perry Stockbridge, "we agree completely."

"Your honor, said Whitman, "may I respond?"

"Sure," said McGarrity.

"First, it's an emergency motion. Movant just came into possession of important information yesterday. We didn't have time to prepare affidavits. Just a bare-bones motion." He turned to face the gallery, turned back. "We do have witnesses here who can testify. Mr. Feinberg here. Mr. McDowell — "

Judge McGarrity interrupted. "That's this Pontiac McDowell? A ... " he pronounced the word with distaste, " ... 'journalist'?"

Spiro laid his hand — firmly — on Pontiac's knee, to keep him in his seat. Pontiac muttered what he usually muttered.

The deputy said, "Hey! Quiet back there!"

Whitman said, "The doctors who testified to Mr. Blauser's incompetence."

Perry quickly interjected, "Here to testify to issues that were not before them in the petition matter."

"And, finally," said Whitman, "Mr. Blauser himself and - ."

Perry said, "He's incompetent. How could he testify?"

Vivian Rucker said, "He can be qualified to testify to facts, your honor."

Whitman said, "And we have the conflicts issue."

"Okay," said the judge. "Here's the way it goes. Let's talk about conflicts before we talk about witnesses. I think that's easier. Just us lawyers. Mr. Stockbridge. Did you do a conflicts check?"

Perry said, "Yes, your honor."

"Well, then," said the judge to Whitman, "there you go. That takes care of that."

"When?" said Rollo, unable to contain himself.

Judge McGarrity glared at Rollo. "Are you a lawyer, sir?"

"No, your honor. I mean, I graduated, but I haven't taken the bar yet. I will this — "

"Well, you have enough of them here, so I don't want to hear from you again. Take a seat. Or take a hike."

Abashed, Rollo sat.

McGarrity watched Rollo and waited until he sat, then fixed his gaze on Perry again. "But it's a good question, so I'll ask it. When?"

Perry said, "Before we agreed to undertake plaintiff's representation in this matter."

Judge McGarrity echoed flatly, "'Before.'"

"Yes," said Perry. "A thorough check."

The judge said, "Since then ... ?"

Perry felt upended at the bench and slammed against it, but he kept his footing. "No."

McGarrity said, "Mr. Blauser was your partner."

"Yes."

"I know that, sir. That wasn't a question. I used to see him in here. You've reviewed the allegations in the motion. Is he still your partner?"

Perry said, "No."

"How do you know that?"

Perry paused before he answered. "He abandoned our practice."

The judge said, "When?"

Perry struggled with this and settled on "Years ago," in a barely audible voice. "More than a decade. I ... I had this issue researched, your honor. We are prepared to brief it."

Judge McGarrity gripped the motion with both hands, looked down at it. "Movant claims ... " with a nod toward Rollo, hunched forward in his chair, " ... sorry, his *guardian* claims, on his behalf, he lacked capacity to abandon the practice. Mr. Blauser."

McGarrity let the paper fall from his hands. "If that's true, and I'm not finding it is, you've been representing a client in an action against one of your own partners."

Wonderingly, McGarrity repeated, "Suing one of your own partners. For one of your clients. An incompetent partner, apparently, but a partner no less. Without," he looked down at the motion, "'without obtaining a waiver of the conflict in representation.' From your client and your partner. 'Without a consent to represent one party notwithstanding the conflict.'" The judge permitted himself to look perplexed. "I mean, if you can get a consent on these facts." He corrected himself. "Allegations. I'm not even sure it's possible. To get a consent." The judge paused, looked down at Perry. "Without even seeking one. Do you see a conflict in that?"

Perry felt the silence grow around and in him, thick and high, filling the courtroom.

The judge said, "Mr. Stockbridge? I said, do you see a conflict? How about the potential for conflict? Or at least an appearance of conflict?"

Perry said, "Your honor, I ... " and stopped. "Yes. Yes, your honor. I see it. All of it. I see the ... entirety of it, now." He turned his head for a moment to find Milton in the gallery. Milton had laid his head on Louise's shoulder and closed his eyes. He gave no sign and every sign of hearing.

David Whitman spoke again. "For the record, your honor. Movant has notified the A.R.D.C. of the professional issues raised by these facts — "

The judge said, "Allegations, counsel. Let's not get ahead of ourselves."

"Yes, your honor, thank you. These allegations. I should note that Mr. Feinberg has today filed a complaint in Chancery against Danville & Williamston — "

In the back of the courtroom, Langdon Danville stood up suddenly. Emmitt Markell just as quickly pulled him down again.

" — seeks an accounting for Mr. Blauser's share of the firm's assets and proceeds, including his partner's share accruing in prior fiscal years."

"Sweet *Christ*," whispered Danville.

Whitman allowed himself a brief smile, continued. "And there's a wild card here. Because of the complexity of Mr. Blauser's affairs, we aren't entirely sure today what Thorn & Texas owns." He paused. "The company or Mr. Blauser, or the two together, may own Mr. Blauser's share of Danville & Williamston."

Judge McGarrity gaped, raised a hand to stop him. "Wait a minute." He flipped the pages of the motion, front to back, back to front. "Did I read something in here about Mr. Stockbridge representing the ... " he scanned the caption, " ... the Lynette Foundation, in an acquisition of Thorn and ... Thorn and ... help me out here."

Whitman said, "Thorn and Texas? Yes, your honor."

"So, Thorn and ... Texas might own a part of the law firm that is representing a client that's trying to acquire Thorn and ... Thorn and whatever." The judge shook his head to clear it. "But a business can't own a law practice, can it? I thought only lawyers could own their law practices."

"Standing here today, your honor? Honestly?" Whitman shrugged. "I can't quite answer that question. We just don't know. Lawyers can own entities that participate in law-firm ownership. Professional corporations, for example."

The judge said, "So it's possible that there are even more conflicts here than we've identified so far. Forgive me. *Potential* conflicts. I am not making any findings here, you understand. Not on this record. Really, there is no record." He looked at Stockbridge, said, "Yet."

"Yes, sir," said Whitman.

"I see that Mr ... . " he looked from Rollo to Whitman, who mouthed, " ... Fanberg, yes, is bursting to speak. You may." He looked up at the clock. "But keep it short."

Rollo stood up and walked up to the bench. "Your honor. Thank you. Milton's incompetent. Well, how *long* do we think he's been, what is it, unfit? I think since Mrs. Stockbridge died. He lost it right there. He couldn't work, couldn't focus, Milton. He couldn't even rouse himself when you, I mean Mr. Stockbridge, left. He kept this book, though. A book on the firm. We think," Rollo said, thumbs pointing to the lawyers at his sides, "he expected an *accounting* someday." He smiled. "I got a letter from him. Asking me to be his guardian. And for an accounting."

"A dissolution of the partnership," said Whitman, "a winding up of its affairs, and an accounting under the Uniform Partnership Act."

"So," said Rollo. "What you got is one pathetic little guy. He's all messed up. He trashes his practice, his career, everything. He's a busboy sleeping in a firetrap on his old case files." Rollo stood silently for a second, recalling his first visit to Milton's. "But, he's keeping this list. Carries it with him wherever he goes. It's up to date through the first of the month. This month."

The judge looked away from Rollo, to Perry. "I suppose you're going to want an evidentiary hearing on all this. And then briefs. And what with everything, with the other complaint, and the A.R. D.C. matter, you're going to want a lot of time. Sixty days for the hearing?"

Perry said, "Ninety."

"Okay, Mr. Whitman?"

Whitman nodded. "So long as the order to vacate is stayed, yes, your honor."

"Oh," said the judge, "the order to vacate is stayed. Trust me. Indefinitely. We'll set a briefing schedule after the hearing." Thinking, if there is a hearing on this mess.

Langdon Danville shook off Markell's grip and rose from his seat. "Your honor?"

Judge McGarrity looked at him. "Oh, it's Mr. Danville. I thought I saw you pop up back there."

"Your honor," said Danville, "may I approach the bench?"

"Oh, sure. Come on up."

Langdon Danville passed through the gate. Rollo's lawyers moved aside. "So the record is absolutely clear, your honor. I want to assure the Court that we will, Danville & Williamston, *I* will make a thorough investigation of this matter. We maintain the highest ethical standards at our firm and — "

Judge McGarrity said, "I understand, Mr. Danville. The court accepts your ... representation ... that you run the business the way you should. But you can stop now. I need to get on to the rest of my docket." He looked at Whitman. "Okay. Prepare an order. I am definitely staying the order to vacate. Make sure that's in there. And the dates for the hearing. After the hearing, we'll set dates for the briefs. In the meantime," said the judge to Perry, "you need to get busy. And don't waste anytime offering up a response to the motion for reconsideration. That's futile. Well, I can't stop you. But ... "

Rollo saw the expression on Perry's face and knew that he'd never practice law, never sue the Police Department, that he'd wasted several years planning his vendetta for no good goddamn reason. He'd have to atone for all of this some way, this assault on Stockbridge's life's work. The man's practice was ghastly, but it was love's labor.

As Rollo left the courtroom, Pontiac said, "I didn't get to talk."

"Yeah," said Todd, "but there isn't another reporter within a hundred feet of the courtroom. So it's all yours, baby. Run with it."

"And you crushed Stockbridge," said Rollo. "*You* did that. Plus, you get to watch what's next." He nodded at Langdon Danville, who walked toward them, looking *full* of purpose.

Pontiac brightened. "That's true, man. That's true." He laughed. "*Fucking* true."

Milton thought, self defense. For a friend, and for Lynette.

Forty-seven

"Don't sweat it." Rollo said graciously to Langdon Danville. "It's a good deal."

Danville erupted in a series of shouted sentences in which the words "preposterous," "deluded," and "outrageous," appeared, popping up again and again like ducks in a carnival shooting gallery.

Eventually, Danville ran down, which was when Rollo said, "Done? Good," and smiled benignly. "Now, how come I'm making this generous offer to you gentlemen? Instead of going through with an accounting. Which is the nuclear option here. You want me to explain it?

"Basically, time flies when you're having fun. Just not enough. Listen:" and Rollo nodded to Whitman, who cleared his throat and began to read from the text of a photocopied case. "Abandonment is a conscious purpose on the part of the owner of personal property so to treat it as to manifest an intention," Rollo's attorney paused and said again "*an intention*, thereafter to neither use it nor retake it into his possession. Abandonment is an intentional relinquishment of a known right."

"In*ten*tion," said Rollo. "What do you need to form intent? *Capacity*, right? But we got Milton. He checks out, *out*, pretty much the second he gets the news about Lynette. Excuse me. Mrs. Stockbridge. And what else do you need to prove intent to abandon?" He nodded again to Whitman, who read this: "Intention must be shown by acts or words or both, but the acts relied on must be of an unequivocal and decisive character."

The two D&W lawyers said nothing. Well, almost nothing. Langdon Danville said, "I invite you to leave. Now."

Rollo sat back, folded his hands on the table. "It's the building for your practice, Mr. Stockbridge. And you don't get Thorn and Texas. Give up Milton's building or we go to the mat for your practice."

Rollo thundered on, laying bloodily about him with fiduciary sword. For Langdon Danville's benefit, Rollo added this: "Maybe we even get a slice of Danville & Williamston. Your letterhead says 'A partnership including professional corporations.' Where does Stockbridge & Blauser end? Where does Danville begin?"

Rollo shrugged cheerfully. "Hey, I sure as heck don't know. But the judge'll tell us what he thinks. If we ask. Maybe we win, maybe we lose. We all roll the dice and watch them bounce along the felt." To his port-side lawyer, Rollo said tersely, "Give them the draft, please."

The attorney handed round copies of a one-page proposed agreement. On that one page, Perry Stockbridge, Lynette's foundation, Danville & Williamston, and their heirs, successors, and assigns, disclaimed all right, title, and interest in Blauser's building and Thorn and Texas. And on that same page, as consideration therefore, Rollo, as fiduciary and trustee for Milton and Thorn and Texas, and for all heirs, successors, and assignees thereof, abandoned all right, title, and interest in Stockbridge & Blauser, Danville & Williamston, and any subsequent practice "formed therefrom or associated therewith."

Reading along with them, Rollo said, "I forgot. You fix what you did to the flake. You know, Brooks. Give the guy a nice apology. Like it was all a big mistake. Put it in his file. And references. A-pluses."

Langdon Danville cleared his throat but still croaked, "You could lose."

Rollo nodded. "Absolutely. No question about it. That's the beauty of the law. But the bad news, *your* bad news, is we could win. Most everyone gets past a motion to dismiss. And we're pretty sure we can beat a motion for summary judgment. Maybe we even *win* on summary judgment. We haven't decided if we can get a jury trial. We asked for one, but sitting here with you today, I'll be honest, we're still working our way through this." Rollo looked up and around him. "But what if we can get a jury? Who's a jury like more? A busboy or a big law firm? We can find out. And I'm telling you, I'm promising you, I'll spend as much as these guys tell me I should. That's my duty to Milton. I can go deep on this. The Nazis only got four million. There's plenty left."

Stockbridge said, "This is untimely."

Rollo nodded, shrugged, said, "We do what we can with what we got." He stood up, looked at his watch. "It's 11:28. What we do is we wait for a call from you by close of business tomorrow. No. Today. You agree, we dismiss with prejudice, subject to our little agreement here. You don't call, or you say no deal, we slap *lis pendens* on everything in this place. Then we got Milton Blauser, *et al*, vs. Perry Stockbridge, *et al*. Messy, public, and endless."

David Whitman said, "We'll oppose any motion to seal the record or close the proceedings."

Rollo nodded, said, "We'll leave you folks to think about it, talk it over." Rollo and his lawyers stood up and left, without handshakes, leaving Stockbridge and Danville in the conference room.

Forty-eight

No single room in Danville and Williamston can hold all of its 118 equity partners at one time, not even the partners' dining room. So, the management committee convened them in the auditorium of the bank that owned the building on which the firm's imaginary shingle hung.

Langdon Danville, Perry Stockbridge and the other three members of D&W's management committee occupied five chairs behind a table on the stage. Partners who were out of town or on vacation were paged and teleconferenced in.

To this audience of wealthy, powerful, and anxious men and women clutching crumpled e-mail messages in their laps, Danville said, "The firm's assets are exposed to an indeterminable amount of risk. It's our view that the risk is unacceptable. We ask you to approve this proposed agreement, as absurdly odious as it is. This unfortunate chapter in the history of our great firm should remind us that every 'i' must be dotted and every 't' crossed. Anyone who brings clients here from another practice must unquestionably sever any and all prior ties. And we must make sure that happens."

The partners approved the agreement by a margin of 68-40. The "nays" came mostly from the litigation group, who saw <u>Blauser v. Stockbridge</u> as nice work if they could get it, especially if they could bill their partners for it.

Danville's use of the first person plural throughout his brief statement was the only consideration Perry asked for, or received, in exchange for resigning that day from the management committee.

And that was *that*.

Forty-nine

Cut loose by D&W, rehabilitated, in again from the cold, Todd could write his book, if he could prise it from the untidy stack of legal pads he'd covered with Milton's story. Or he could practice law again. Or study origami or tend bar or do just about any other damn thing he could think of.

But Todd needed to think carefully, *judiciously*, about what he wanted to be when he grew up. And *darn* that pesky threshhold question! Did he *want* to grow up? Todd craved respect, but only grownups got real respect, grownups like Louise recumbent at his side, and children of adversity, mature and wise beyond their years, and old people who got through their disasters with their dignity, hope and humor intact. Todd conceded he was (d), none of the above.

On the other hand, if Todd wrote his book and sold it and got rich, he was pretty certain he'd get respect *without* growing up, like celebrities frozen in pop-eyed, makeup-free stupefaction on the magazine racks in supermarket check-out lines. Todd liked that possibility, but it was only that — a possibility, a long-shot, even with a tail wind.

Because his interminable, unfocussed note-making on Blauser reminded Todd that writing is *work*, which is what grown-ups do *all* the fucking time, except for celebrities who farmed out their memoirs to as-told-to-ologists. "This," Todd said to Louise, "is a conundrum." Todd loved that word. "I want respect, but I have to work for respect, but I don't want to work."

"Conundrum boy," murmured Louise into his shoulder, "You want to lie on a chaise, eating bonbons and reading photo magazines."

"Looking *at* photo magazines," Todd corrected her. "One doesn't read them. Except in supermarket lines."

"Or in a metaphor," Louise replied. Inhaling, swinging for the fences, she said, "You could be my house spouse."

"What," asked Todd, distracted by a rough bump that was the mole on her left shoulder blade.

Louise raised up from lying against him. She pressed an index finger against her lips and touched it to his. "If you listened, really listened," she said, "I bet you'd never say 'what?'"

"Really," Todd asked, wonderingly. "Never?"

"Never," Louise assured him. "Listening enables you to hear what other people say to you. For example ... "

"Yes?"

" ... if you were listening, you heard me propose to you."

"You did? When?"

Louise did not answer.

"Now I'm listening," Todd said plaintively, "but you're not saying anything."

"Oh, but I am."

"What?" asked Todd.

"Nothing," said Louise.

"You're saying nothing, and I'm listening carefully to your silence. It's getting way too zen in here for me. The sound of one hand clapping is deafening."

Louise sighed. This would take longer than she'd expected, but Todd appeared to be a ready and willing student. He had not yet proved to be able, but much evidence, Louise believed (with the generous great patience of any woman who loves any man), remained to be put in.

Fifty

"Flies in the ointment," Milton muttered to himself, frowning at a printout of Thorn and Texas transactions. "Motes in the eye of the mind."

The new security system for Milton's building beeped. Rollo looked up at the little monitor over the door and saw Perry Stockbridge standing alone on the stoop. Rollo buzzed him in, stepped outside Milton's apartment to wait on the landing.

As he climbed the stairs, Perry saw Rollo and said, "The sword and the shield. May I speak with him?"

Rollo looked at his watch. "Visiting hours're over." Perry turned to descend the stairs and Rollo said quickly, "It's a joke. I'm his guardian. Not the warden."

"You miss the mark with that false humility," said Perry as he edged past Rollo into the apartment. Perry saw Milton on the couch and said to Rollo, "May I speak with him alone?"

As Rollo weighed the chances that there might be violence, Perry said, "You can search me if you want to."

Rollo shrugged and said, "You're not going to hurt him." He carried a chair out to the landing and closed the door behind him.

Perry also took a chair and positioned it next to the couch. He sat, hands on his knees, and gazed at Milton. Perry said, "Lynette charged you to cultivate her gift, but you won't use it. But if you're incompetent, a guardian can spend that money for you. Deploy it wisely on your behalf. Feinberg spends it for you. He makes all the choices you can't make. All the right choices." Perry smiled. "I see the beauty in it."

But there was "No game here," mumbled Milton. "No false front."

"I acknowledge that," said Perry equably. "You have to be mad to prevail. That's why we want you at the firm. Come back. We offer an inexhaustible supply of complex problems."

"Too busy," Milton said quickly, waving a hand sharply, dismissively. "Too busy."

Perry leaned in toward Milton and lowered his voice to a whisper. "I am ... incomplete without you. In that place. I have always been. I don't want to feel unfinished anymore."

"Study the past," Milton said. "Solve the past."

Stockbridge weighed this, fairly. He said, "I'm no good at that. I get on with things." He paused, added, "But I won't ask you to."

Fifty-one

" ... and here you are," said the Peach. "I *am* surprised. Did you bring the albums?"

"Yes," said Perry, taking them out of his briefcase and handing them to her.

"Let's have a look at them." She smiled shyly. "After we visit a bit. As a means to getting on with things."

Fifty-two

Sixteen months of arduous negotiations secured the rights to all of the parts of the story related here. Louise's linchpin acquisition was the Peach's work, which Perry consented to produce on the birth day of his daughter.

Pontiac exhorted Todd to seize the genre, *any* genre, by the *throat*, and gratify his readers' basest urges. Near the end, however, chastened, and just exactly here, Todd wrote only that Milton was who he was and that's all who he was, like the cartoon sailor singing at that moment, in fluid 1930s black and white animation on the six-inch color television screen perched on the far arm of Milton's couch. In Milton's *home*.

Really, the equation was simple. If Milton were sane he'd be homeless. But he was, what? "Homeful," Milton whispered to himself. "I am homeful."

Oblivious to Milton's grateful homeful calculus on the couch behind him, Rollo shivered in the January wind leaking through the walls. He pulled the phone and yellow pages to him, pushed his glasses up on his nose. He ordered double-glazed, no, *triple-glazed*, windows and blown-in insulation, and tuck-pointing, to complement the new furnace cranking away in the basement of Blauser's ancient building.

The good thing about winter, Rollo reminded himself, the only good thing, was the dog's crap froze in the backyard and he could pick it up using a plastic supermarket bag wrapped around his hand as a glove, no problem, and jam it cleanly into a second bag in his other hand.

And the frozen crap didn't stink. There was no odor of decay.

And speaking of crap, Rollo thought, remarking sixteen inches of junk mail on the table before him. One week's accumulation attracted by Milton's wealth. Rollo dumped these into the large plastic garbage can beside him. Then he opened the more substantial pieces, starting with a large manilla envelope with bubble padding. The return address on it was a post-office box number in Atlanta. Out of the envelope, Rollo pulled a framed photograph, a black-and-white pose of two men standing on either side of a woman with her hands on the push-bar of a stroller in front of her.

Rollo — the trained detective — identified the men easily and immediately: they were Stockbridge and Blauser. He inferred that the woman was Lynette, because Stockbridge had an arm draped casually over her shoulder.

The three adults were smiling. In the stroller, there was a small sleeping boy in a tee shirt, shorts, and sandals over socks. A balloon floated up from a string knotted around his tiny wrist. The child's chin rested on his chest, head tilting off to the right side at an impossible angle that only supple young children can achieve without injury.

End

Denlinger's Publishers, Ltd. —"The book publisher for tomorrow's great authors... today!" —hopes you have enjoyed reading this book.

We will forward your emailed comments to the author upon request. [support@thebookden.com].

Visit our on-line bookstore for additional titles.

http://www.thebookden.com

Mission Statement

We will earnestly strive to enrich and entertain our customers through reading by promoting one of our constitutional rights, "freedom of speech." And, with honesty and integrity, strive to recognize and promote authors by publishing their works.

Denlinger's Publishers & Bookstore
P.O. Box 1030 – Edgewater, FL 32132-1030